Ulrike Dietmann

Medicine Horse

Volume 1: Initiation

spiritbooks

© 2013 spiritbooks, 73230 Kirchheim/Teck, Germany
Publisher: spiritbooks, www.spiritbooks.de
Author: Ulrike Dietmann
Cover illustration: Kim McElroy, www.spiritofhorse.com
Cover design: Martin Roser
Printing and publisher's service provider: www.tredition.de
Printed in Germany
ISBN: 978-3-944587-00-4

All events and characters in this novel are fictional. Any similarities to actual events or persons living or dead are purely coincidental.

For my Shooting Stars: Martin, Joel, Lea
For Tinnia, the whispering horse
For Gitanes, the mystery

1

"Read *that*", said Mrs Barzi.

The small red-haired woman with the name that reminded Valerie of warts and witches had simply pulled the book out of her handbag and let it slide into Valerie's hand like a cold fish. Valerie's resistance was too weak to say: no. She had met Mrs Barzi several times in the street or, like now, in the baker's shop. And each time the Wart had greeted her as if they knew one another, but that was not the case. There was a sort of death rattle in her breathing and she looked in general so fragile, that Valerie would not have managed to reject a present from her anyway.

She would have liked to know what kind of book it was, but a thick, blue dust-jacket covered it as if its identity were too dangerous to reveal in Schlattstall, this dump of a place at the end of the world.

Mrs Barzi smiled conspiratorially.

"Looks interesting," said Valerie and smiled back. Curious the baker's wife glanced knowingly across her row of Chelsea buns. There was an atmosphere as if they were all part of a secret mission with its epicentre here in Schlattstall of all places: this scattered heap of houses surrounded by three dark, steep slopes which resolutely hid from the eyes of the world everything that happened here. Perhaps, Valerie thought, real conspiracies could only ever thrive in a place like this, or perhaps it was simply that her poor reason—shattered in a thousand pieces—had once more got the better of her.

Mrs Barzi went on death rattling and Valerie squinted. Her eyes had been inflamed since the day somebody had snatched her out of her body without putting her back properly: three months earlier, going by the earth time scale—but, then again, who went by that?

"Good-bye," Valerie said.

Once home she opened the book at random:

Problems of the eye, the gateway to the soul, indicate that you do not want to see something important.

That's just it, thought Valerie, ha-ha, and again her eyes started to itch like crazy. Glaring light poured in through the south window so she closed the blinds until only thin strips penetrated the dents in the slats. She opened the terrace door for Miou. The grey cat sidled round Valerie's ankles and curled its tail round her carves. The pain in her eyes stung like a thousand needles.

The phone rang. Valerie froze. Something—she felt it exactly—was lurking in the left-hand corner of the room, then it leapt to the phone and screamed: Pick it up! way Valerie was determined not to give in to this ghost which had settled in her house without being invited. She lit a candle on the chest of drawers and watched a gnat fly towards the flame. Her heart clenched.

On no account, she thought, may I open the door to my soul to see something important, for if I do, I will be burnt up like this poor insect.

Valerie stared at the charred remains of the gnat and was overwhelmed with pity, she wanted to lie down and die with the defenceless creature.

Where was the poor insect's soul now? Was it where Miriam's soul was? She closed her eyes and a flood-tide of images came rolling in. She could not remember ever having had such wild imaginings as she'd had since September 23rd. Gory battles raged, she saw horses bolting in panic, a gathering of holy men and a landscape of vast steppes. A horse disentangled itself from the raging flood of images and told her his name. She considered writing the name down, and with trembling fingers searched for a pen in the chest of drawers. Too tired to sit in a chair she dropped to the floor, leant with her back against the sofa and tugged a piece of newspaper towards her to scribble the horse's name in the margin.

Massacre in Arizona, read the headline of an article in the paper and it seemed to her as if there was some strange connection between this article and her flood of images. That's it, she thought, and drew a ring round the headline.

She was just about to write down the horse's name when a wave of sweet bliss washed over her and she had the feeling that she was stepping outside her body just like that day when ... Write! Write!! she told her hand. But it was so good to swim around out there, basking in the feeling of bliss and she wanted to savour it for a while. She was so tired ... so tired ... Sleep overwhelmed her.

When she woke up again, it was dark outside and the candle had almost burnt down. She reached for the newspaper and saw to her amazement that along the edge something really was written:

A horse named Gitanes
A black and white Berber paint
his head reminiscent of an Indian

2

"Yes?" Valerie held the receiver away as if she was instinctively expecting something unpleasant.

"Your daughter's locker..."

Valerie could not answer.

"Will you come over?... or shall we throw the things away?"

That something in the left-hand corner hopped about like a hobgoblin. It taunted gloatingly:

You'll die.

"I'll come."

Before Valerie set off, she removed the protective cover from the book Mrs Barzi had given her and read the title: *Conversations with the Dead.*

The smell of horse manure assailed Valerie's nostrils and the itching in her eyes became unbearable. She had never liked horses: not in the past and now even less. She would have liked nothing better than to turn round and run away. A pretty girl with large dark eyes and long chestnut-brown hair was leading a black horse across the yard. The girl turned round, Valerie had the feeling that the girl, who was about thirteen, was reading her thoughts. Perhaps she had been one of Miriam's friends.

It took Valerie all her strength to push the wooden barn door open, but the effort jolted her back to the present. A dog came leaping towards her, she jumped and thrust the animal away, it smelled of wet hair.

Miriam had once shown her the locker right at the beginning when she had taken on the gigantic horse she was sharing. *I didn't spend enough time in the stable with Miriam, hardly any,* Valerie thought, *because I loathe horses. I never took Miriam's love of horses seriously. But then how could I? They are dangerous, potentially lethal. It's inconceivable to spend any time near them. I was a bad mother.*

On the back of the locker door was a photograph of the giant, one of the ugliest horses Valerie had ever seen. He was called 'Korbas'. An ugly horse with an even uglier name. It was all so inconceivable.

The locker door made a metallic sound when Valerie yanked it open. Miriam's riding helmet fell out and rolled across the floor. She picked it up and stroked it gently as if she could compensate for something by doing that. On the shelves she found a pair of riding gloves made of brown leather, cowboy boots size 35, a bag of horse food, a tin of hoof polish with its brush, a hoof scraper, a large and a small grooming brush. To touch the objects, Valerie thought with a shock, feels like touching Miriam or what Miriam now was.

Valerie grasped the hoof scraper with her fingers, clutching involuntarily until her knuckles were white. This plastic orange currycomb with its bent and twisted bristles was the only connection she still had to Miriam.

The door to the tack room burst open with a brutal push because it jammed, and a delicate woman with a floppy hat and thin light-brown hair came in. Over her flowery blouse she was wearing a crocheted jacket that made her look rather quaint as if she had just popped out of a children's book.

"You are Miriam's mother?" the stranger asked, and again Valerie had the unpleasant feeling that somebody was reading her thoughts. She stuffed the hoof scraper into a cloth bag as if she had been caught doing something forbidden.

"I can imagine what you are thinking," said the children's book character. Since when had anyone invited her to say anything?

No, you can't, thought Valerie and stared at the ground. She found herself peering at a pair of turquoise crocodile cowboy boots with pointed toes and stitched seams?

"Miriam waited for you," said the cross between cowgirl and Mary Poppins.

"What do you mean?"

"Just what I said."

"I don't understand."

"Yes, you do."

Valerie found the answer rude and much too private.

"Please, leave me alone now. This is all very difficult for me."

"If you want somebody to talk to, here's my card."

Anger surged inside Valerie. This stranger was looking for customers at a time like this. That was why she had come. She wanted to take advantage of the situation. Valerie ignored the outstretched hand and the card, and turned back to the locker. Behind her she heard the woman leave the room, leaving behind a strange mood like a sticky cloud. Valerie felt as if she was hanging from a pendulum and swinging back and forth between two worlds, each more unreal than the other.

For a moment Valerie was even wondering whether this woman had actually been here in the tack room at all, or whether she had merely imagined the whole thing. Since Miriam's accident every possible phenomenon—each one blurring the edges of reality beyond recognition—had occupied her mind. Valerie's glance leapt to the feeding box where the violet card lay: proof that the lady had actually been there. Valerie didn't manage to read the card because at that very moment the girl she had met in the yard, accompanied by a friend, appeared in the doorway. Valerie quickly stowed the card in the rear pocket of her jeans.

From the furthest back corner of the locker she extracted a postcard and blew the dust off it. It showed a black-and-white-piebald horse. The words she had noted down came to mind again. She turned the postcard over and there, in Miriam's childlike handwriting, were the words: *a horse called Gitanes.* Valerie felt dizzy. On the edge of the card in small letters was printed the horse's breed: *Berber paint mix.* She looked at the horse and thought of the fourth line of what she had noted down: *his head is reminiscent of an Indian.* She studied the horse's head and discovered that it actually did have something of an Indian about it.

She cleared out the locker completely, also took the saddle, the bridle tack and the half-empty bag of food and stowed it all away in the boot of her car. She couldn't bring herself to take the things into the house. Somehow the boot seemed to be a suitable place for Miriam's belongings, a mobile twilight zone.

At home Valerie flicked through a box of horse postcards from a shelf in Miriam's room. She would have given anything for an explanation of the strange overlap between her notes and the postcard in Miriam's locker. Surely she had already seen the card with the black-and-white paint horse before Miriam had taken it with her to the stable and that's why it had come to mind by chance. Perhaps Miriam had also shown her the card and told her that she would take it with her, although Valerie could not remember that. She discovered a series of cards which depicted various horse breeds, to which the card with the *Berber* also belonged. If she had actually seen the card lying around, perhaps she had had it in her hand when tidying up—in that case the precision of the human memory was astonishing. How else could she have known a black-and-white piebald *Berber*, when she didn't even know there was such a breed as *Berber*.

How on earth could one explain the horse's name *Gitanes* otherwise. She had probably also read the name *Gitanes* while tidying up, her subconscious had taken to the name *Gitanes*, 'gypsy' in English, because even as a child she had wanted to travel around with the gypsies—and so it had found its way to the front shelf in the great archive of her subconscious. Such things were probably normal for psychologists, therapists, clairvoyants. She put the card back in its box with the other cards. The explanation about the unconscious appealed to her more and more the longer she thought about it.

To get rid of the irritating odour of the stable exuding from her jeans and her pullover she went into the bedroom and changed her clothes. As she slid her jeans over her hips, the visiting card of the woman with the floppy hat fell from her rear pocket and lay, reverse side up, on the carpet. Something had been noted down on it by hand. Valerie bent down. Scrawled on it was: *Gitanes.* Valerie's thoughts froze.

3

Reason told her she ought to talk to somebody, to a person who understood her situation, but she could not muster the energy to phone anybody. Her reason also told her that this somebody should on no account wear turquoise crocodile cowboy boots.

The wind toyed with the mobile hanging in the apple tree, producing an angelic tinkling sound. Valerie bit into an orange, licked her fingers clean and had the feeling that the orange was turquoise.

Now that Miriam was no longer there, it occurred to her that for years she had been neglecting her friendships and that there was hardly any person she was on intimate terms with left in her life. Nobody phoned to ask how she was; she had had a mere five cards of condolence: one from Miriam's school class, three from distant friends and one from the new parish priest whom she had never met.

Miou jumped onto her lap, sorted her limbs according to some invisible geometry then relaxed completely. "You are the only one I still have," Valerie said and stroked the cat's grey fur. That afternoon she once more gave in to the telephone ringing. "We haven't heard from you for weeks." It was her sister, Tamara of the grating voice.

"I've heard nothing from you either," replied Valerie weakly.

"Are you OK?" Tamara asked.

"Absolutely," replied Valerie.

"Can you bring a cake? Better still: two. One with buttercream and alcohol and something dry for the children, something they can hold in their hands." The calendar caught Valerie's eye. What day was it today?

"You are coming, aren't you?"

If I haven't flown off on a witch's broom by then, thought Valerie. The idea of celebrating her mother's birthday within the family seemed to her to be as alien as a space ship landing on a cake plate.

"How are you? You know I want the truth. I know what's up anyway."

For a moment Valerie considered telling Tammy about the multiple occurrence of the name *Gitanes* and the hoof scraper which presented a connection with the realm of the dead.

"I'm getting on fine as always," she said.

"Liar."

"Leave me in peace, Tammy, I'm OK."

"It'll do you good to be amongst people."

Sure, Valerie thought.

"Lunch is at half past twelve... Will you be wearing black?"

"No."

"Are you working?"

"Everything's fine, Tammy." She slammed down the receiver.

She thought about how she had always had to blackmail Miriam with riding lessons to get her to come to family celebrations. Ten riding lessons for Auntie Leonie's birthday last year. Valerie felt ashamed at the thought. Nobody there notices me and nobody listens to me, Miriam had complained. They treat me as if I were invisible.

Valerie spent the rest of the day acquiring the makings of a lemon cake and a Black Forest cherry cake. As she was sprinkling flour, baking powder and sugar onto the mixing board, she heard Miriam's voice as if she were sitting there, right next to her on a stool, weighing sugar and flour and beating eggs. 'The flour is the dragon which lays the eggs. It feeds the eggs with baking powder, so they will grow big and strong.' Valerie carefully tipped the yokes into the hollow. 'Then it blows sugar onto the eggs, so they'll have something to munch.'

Valerie deeply regretted that she had agreed to go. She knew that her family was unable to cope with Miriam's death and would do anything to find a guilty party—and an explanation. They would say something ugly. With a knife Valerie cut up the butter just like a dragon battling a fire-spitting monster.

As she was attacking the baking board, she again thought about the crazy woman with the crocodile-leather boots. Valerie strode into the bedroom. The visiting card lay on the little African table next to her bed, still reverse-side up. Valerie turned the card over. It read: Evi Schaefer, *Shamanic Life Guidance*, together with a telephone number. Next to it: a picture of a rainbow-coloured horse. Shamanic life guidance, Valerie thought, but had no idea what it meant.

After she had taken the cake base out of the oven, she doused it with alcohol and covered it with cherries. She put the layers of Black Forest cake together and thought about the quotation in the book from Mrs Barzi about eyes and what they do not wish to see. She coated the whole cake with cream till it was completely covered, then she sprinkled it with chocolate chips.

"Hello Tom." Valerie said, giving her father a fleeting hug. She and Tamara had been using their parents' Christian names for a long time. It had been Tamara's idea; she was determined to be grown up, and Valerie had played along because "Mummy" and "Daddy" sounded to her like army ranks.

"How are you?" her father asked and took her coat. Without waiting for an answer Tom shunted her along the hall and into the living room.

Valerie's mother had as always overdone her make-up and was wearing a check blouse and drainpipe trousers with a broad buckle-belt. She had got it into her head to play the American-style country girl even though she had grown up in Berlin and had spent most of her life in cities. She had brought the idea back from a holiday in the American West. A few years before she had persuaded Tom to buy a house in a village and a dog as well. In the meantime they had three: Great Danes.

They were badly trained and came charging at Valerie. Her mother bossed them about—which had not the slightest effect on them. With people her method was more successful—which also raised an interesting question possibly worth following up.

Tamara stretched out one arm to hug Valerie, while in her other hand she balanced a spoonful of vanilla mousse which she then popped into her mouth.

"You don't know how happy I am to see you. I should have been concerned about you much earlier. You look awful."

Fortunately Tamara had *not* bothered about her sooner. To be taken care of by Tamara was like being hung on a meat hook and spun round.

"I will make up for it," her sister added. "Don't look so horrified. You know I can scan you perfectly." Tamara had made a great career in the personnel department of a technology company and boasted that she only needed to see a person once to be able to tell whether they would make a profit for the company or cost it money. She liked to claim that her x-ray eyes were incorruptible. Right now she was busy scanning Valerie.

"You have to drink mugwort tea," she said after an alarmingly long pause. She wandered into the kitchen and searched through her mother's cupboards. "I've found something even better." She tapped Valerie on the shoulder and handed her an open box of dried dates. Valerie looked at the sell-by-date. It had overrun by two years.

"Since when have you been functioning as a dietary consultant?" Valerie asked.

Tamara ran the spoon with the vanilla cream slowly and with relish over her lower lip. "I've done a course," she said triumphantly.

Valerie slipped the dates unnoticed into the waste bin. Tamara had already lost interest in the subject. She knew nothing about people. Certainly not about me anyway, Valerie thought. It is a good job I didn't give in to the temptation to tell her about the horse postcard. Even if my most urgent need is to find somebody who can provide some explanation or other that I can live with.

Throughout the meal Valerie felt as if any moment a hoof scraper might drop from above and plop into the soup bowl. At the extended dining table sat her parents, Tamara and her husband Mark (who tended towards violence), her brother Leif and his wife, Selma, as well as their three children. Valerie didn't know what to fear more: the conversation at the table or the hoof scraper.

"I hope they shot the horse the same day," said Mark in the silence which had set in after the soup. Mark was not only potentially violent but also an insufferable know-all who wore too much gold jewellery. "What did you say the nag's name was?"

"Korbas," said Mathilde, Selma's ten-year-old daughter, who also loved horses.

"They *did* shoot it," Mark insisted.

"No," said Valerie

"That killing machine's still alive? Tell me where he is and I'll blow his brains out. You shoot horses between the ears, don't you?"

The idea seemed to amuse Mark. Valerie could no longer stand it and got up from her seat. She was involuntarily struck by guilty feelings about Miriam's death, but on the other hand, how could she feel at home in a family where a character like Mark had found a nesting place?

"Where are you going?" asked her mother, who reacted like a seismograph to mood swings.

"To the toilet."

As Valerie came back along the hall, she heard the family talking.

"If you ask me, she is ready for the loony bin. Another month alone in that house and we can have her taken away. We really must do something, and I mean ..."

"Valerie is too intelligent to have anyone tell her what to do."

"I will see to it that the horse is shot," said Mark.

Valerie's stomach contracted like a piece of dry bread. I ought to go, she thought, and had the feeling that her reason had at last returned. One beat later her reason told her that a sudden departure would cause too much commotion, so that possibly they might *really* come and take her away.

She sat down in her seat again and placed the serviette on her knees. Tamara then said: "I'd like to tell you all what I've been thinking since ... I don't know when, never mind, don't take offense, but it needs to be said ... I wasn't surprised that Miriam died." She put on a conspiratorial voice.

I knew it, thought Valerie, I just knew someone would say something hateful. Perhaps it would even be good to be put in the nut house, maybe there they treat one another more humanely.

"How could you?" shouted Valerie's mother indignantly.

"Let me finish, Mum, just this once." Valerie could not remember Tamara ever having had too little chance to talk.

"Miriam was not ... normal. We all knew that and ..."

"The child is dead!"

"Miriam was a ghost," Tamara went on undeterred. "Whenever she walked into the room, I felt there was a ghost coming in. Even now I sometimes feel she is still here. My blood freezes just talking about her ... After all I'm sensitive to such things and I know what I'm talking about. Yes, even if that shocks you, I need to get it off my chest. In my opinion Miriam was a ghost. She had the life span of a ghost and after all that's limited. She no longer liked it here and she has slipped into a different body as ghosts do."

"Interesting," Valerie said, feeling she had internally suffered a burst water pipe.

"Hang on, I'm not finished yet," Tamara drew breath. Her voice coiled itself like a predator before it leaps. "And Valerie is possessed by the ghost of her dead child. That happens and more often than people tend to think. Can't you see the rings under her eyes, ... the absent gaze, the slowed movements. What Valerie needs is not a psychiatrist but an exorcist."

Valerie was speechless. This was by far the most impressive demonstration of so-called knowledge of human nature that Tamara had ever produced.

Being insulted by her sister wouldn't have mattered to Valerie but that she insulted Miriam was going too far. She wanted to burst into the room, rip her sister's head off and tear her into a thousand tiny pieces. She owed it to Miriam but her throat was totally dry. I really am ill, she thought, otherwise I'd declare World War III. She couldn't utter a single word. Her eyes were burning like mad and she was blinking uncontrollably. Her sister-in-law's baby started to cry.

"That was totally out of order," her mother said.

"I expect you to apologize to your sister," Tom said.

"I'm a grown woman. I say what I think, I don't care how others take it," Tamara replied vehemently.

"Good of you to come," said Tom in farewell. "I know how sad you feel." He hugged Valerie. "I only wish I could comfort you."

"Thank you, Tom."

"Now you come to mention it, I've met a man in the fitness studio, who's also called Tom."

"How do you mean: Tom?"

"Haven't you mentioned someone called Tom?" her father asked.

"No," Valerie answered, astonished. "I don't know any Tom."

"He trains at the same time as I do, a friendly, pleasant person. Looks a bit like an Indian. He doesn't talk rubbish like most people. It turns out that we not only have the same name but the same birthday: May 23rd. Isn't that odd?"

Valerie found it comforting that other people also experienced strange coincidences. Even somebody as sober as her father, who had worked in a bank all his life.

"He's American or has American parents. As I said, his face reminds me a bit of an Indian ..."

4

Evi Schaefer—Shamanic Life Guidance ... Valerie had not slept for three days. Her eyes hurt so much that every few seconds she closed them tight, her heart was beating so wildly that she had the feeling the fuse would soon be burnt right down and the bomb in her chest would explode. There was a deathly silence in the house, even the birds seemed to have been struck dumb. Throughout the neighborhood everybody seemed to have died, Valerie had seen nobody for three days. Perhaps the whole of humanity has died out, Valerie thought, except I haven't noticed it yet.

Something in her resisted phoning the person with the floppy hat. What could be the use of a shamanic life guide apart from giving her totally confused reason the final kick over the edge of mental sanity? On the other hand who else was there, dear hoof scraper?

In the afternoon the snow was falling so heavily that Valerie thought it was snowing in her body, covering her arteries, so that she would be turned to ice from within. Sooner or later they would find her, her body leaning against the hot radiator, frozen to death.

"I knew you would phone me," said the voice at the other end. "But I thought you would do it sooner. You seem to have strong nerves." Valerie didn't like the reproachful tone in Evi Schaefer's voice at all.

"How do you mean?"

"You're living dangerously. Perhaps you're simply irresponsible."

"What are you talking about?" Valerie regretted having phoned. I should have guessed that Evi Schaefer is mad. That'll be my downfall.

"I know what you're thinking," Evi replied.

"What are your fees and when can you see me?" Valerie asked.

"Come tomorrow afternoon at three o'clock. I charge 50 Euros an hour."

Valerie was relieved that Evi Schaefer had a price. That gave the whole thing a touch of normality.

"OK".

The house was hardly recognizable from the street. A chestnut tree and a line of gloomy pine trees hid the facade and only allowed a narrow passage through to some worn-down stone steps. At the top Valerie saw that a field spread out behind the house. She noticed sheep and a large brown horse that turned its head to her curiously.

Evi stood in the doorway in a full-length, earth-coloured skirt and had her hair pinned back in a ponytail. Around her neck there dangled necklaces hung with metal animals, representing a snake, an owl, a deer and Sponge Bob.

She lead Valerie into a room with a large window overlooking the valley, the view, however, was partly restricted by the pine trees. Beyond a side window stood a cherry tree with a birdhouse in it. A cat lay rolled up on the window sill. In a wall of exposed stonework there was a fireplace with a fire burning in it and on the walls there hung carpets with Indian designs, photographs of sunsets and horses, a drum, several rattles and a poster for *Matrix* with Keanu Reeves. Evi Schaefer showed Valerie to a sofa covered with woolen blankets, as she herself sank into a worn, leather chair.

"How are you?" asked Evi. "Would you like a cup of tea?"

"Lousy—is my answer to the first question. Yes, I would love a cup of tea."

"Mugwort," Evi said.

Valerie remembered that Tamara had also wanted to foist mugwort tea on her.

"Yes, fine."

Valerie decided to come straight to the point. "I'm a journalist. I believe in things that I can see and which can be explained scientifically."

"But that's not why you've come to me," answered Evi. Her skin was snow white and her expression could change from one moment to the next into something completely different.

"Why mugwort tea?" Valerie asked.

"For days your house elf has been on to me about your eyes. It's his idea."

Valerie decided to ask no further searching questions.

Evi disappeared into the kitchen and returned with a tray which she had apparently already prepared. She poured tea into a mug.

"Sugar?"

"No, thank you." Valerie raised the cup to her lips and noticed that her hands were shaking. "For some time I have been playing with the idea of contacting a therapist with experience in mourning," Valerie said and tightened her lips. It required an effort of will for her to talk to a stranger about her most painful feelings.

"I'm a journalist and a non-fiction editor," she continued. "I have edited several books by therapists and have actually met them, which gave me the impression that I could not expect any help from that direction ... I hate horses."

"Because a horse killed your daughter?"

"I have seen that you have a horse," said Valerie. "What's its name?"

"Blossom," said Evi.

That really sounds quite normal, thought Valerie.

She told Evi Schaefer about the postcard with the paint horse named Gitanes. "I have never felt attracted to horses, unlike other people, ... unlike Miriam."

"Have you ever had a bad experience with horses?"

"No, I grew up in town and I have never had anything to do with horses."

"It wasn't until Miriam ... that horses came into your life?"

"Did you know Miriam?" Valerie asked.

"Oh yes." Something curiously unspoken resonated in this "oh yes", as if there was a whole story behind it. Valerie realized that her heart was no longer beating quite so loudly.

"What can I do for you?" asked Evi.

"I haven't a clue ... Miriam was an unusual child ... She inhabited a world which remains closed to most people. Through her death I feel for the first time that I am able to look into that strange reality which always separated me from her."

Evi nodded silently. She had curled up cat-like on the sofa, as if she wanted to lend circular form to her energy.

"What you can do for me," Valerie said and gathered all her courage, "I would like to get to know this world because I have the feeling that that's what Miriam wants. It may sound crazy but it seems to me that she has laid a trail with this postcard."

Valerie didn't know whether what she had said made any sense, whether this strange fairy-tale figure had something to offer her apart from hocus-pocus or impertinent callousness.

Evi sighed. She probably sensed Valerie's skepticism. "You must understand ..."

"I understand that it's difficult. It will probably be impossible to introduce me to something for which I will have to ignore the limits of my rational world view ... For me it is unbearable to move outside established reality. But since Miriam's death I have the feeling, ... I can't find my way back into myself, do you understand that? ... I feel totally helpless."

"I don't believe that you are so inaccessible ..."

"Oh yes, I am! I'm an outright rationalist, an atheist, left the church at eighteen, I have never been interested in mysticism, the occult, telepathy or anything of that sort ... Whenever it's a question of having to believe in something instead of being given proof, I opt out ...

In my opinion the human need to believe in a higher power has brought humanity a great deal of unhappiness. Our reason is, after all, our greatest gift."

"You are a mother."

"I *was* a mother." Pain surged through Valerie's veins like liquid fire. "You're right, I still am," she corrected herself. "I always will be." Producing the next sentence felt like pole vaulting. "Three days ago, when you came into the tack room and spoke to me, it seemed as if you had just come on my account. Is that right?"

"Do you believe that?"

"No, of course not, I don't consider myself so important ..."

Evi smiled meaningfully. "I knew you would be in the tack room."

"Of course, you saw me going in. And what should I have been doing but sorting out what my daughter had left behind? I imagined it all, the mystical feeling that I had at our first meeting. I'm drowning in grief, my mind is going berserk, that's why I'm clinging to abstruse things."

"Miriam was there with you, wasn't she?" Evi said.

Valerie felt strangely exposed.

"The things," she heard herself answer, "the things triggered a strong memory in me, the orange hoof scraper ..." Valerie jolted. Outside the window a dark brown horse had appeared with a long white blaze. It was standing behind the fence and looking straight into the room. His expression was full of sympathy—Valerie had never before seen such a look in a horse's eyes. She hadn't expected the horse to come so close to the house. The setting sun bathed the horse's mane in orange light. Valerie swallowed. Without her intending it the words, which for months she hadn't been able to express to anybody, came gushing out of her.

"I haven't wept a single tear since Miriam's death," she said. "My eyes are completely dried up. That's the reason I'm here. I haven't shown any natural expressions of mourning as a mother should have. I don't believe anybody can understand what's going on inside me. I wouldn't expect that from anybody either ... I love my daughter more than anything else ... I only wish I could cry but I can't. My whole body is hurting but I can't feel the grief."

Evi sighed as if she were struggling to say something that she had perhaps not intended. "That day in the stable," she said, "Miriam sent you a message which answers your question and all other questions. Not only did she show you a way but ..."

"How do you mean?"

"She sent you a medicine horse."

"A medicine horse?"

"The horse called Gitanes, the black-and-white Berber paint with the Indian head."

Valerie remembered that Evi knew the name Gitanes, but where had she got all the other details from? Suddenly Valerie felt the coldness of indescribable fear.

"How come you know all that?" she asked.

Valerie noticed some movement in the corner of her eye, and when she looked up she saw under an overhanging branch a second horse next to the brown one pushing itself forward. It was black-and-white and its head looked Indian. Valerie felt as if reality were dissolving around her and she would be floating any minute.

"W-w-where's the horse come from?" she stammered.

"It's a Berber-paint-mix that came to me six months ago."

"A Berber?" Valerie's mouth was so dry that she croaked. "He belongs to you?"

"He belongs to a man called Tom."

"Tom?"

"A half-breed Indian."

"Tom, a half-breed Indian? ... The horse came to you six months ago, you say?"

"Yes. Tom brought it to me. He said it's a medicine horse and I would need it."

"What for?"

"For you, Valerie ..."

5

In the night after her visit to Evi Schaefer's Valerie dreamt of a large white ship on which a woman suffering from asthma was travelling.

For two days she thought about her experience at Evi Schaefer's. She had not made a new appointment, everything was too monstrous, seemed to her like a conspiracy against her that somebody or other had brought to life: Evi, this paint horse and a man named Tom were all involved. On the third day Valerie knew why she had to see Evi again.

"I don't wish to be impolite, but I hate this mugwort tea."

"It is wonderful for bronchial and lung complaints."

"My lungs feel quite normal." Valerie thought of the dream about the woman with asthma.

Evi smiled impenetrably.

"I've come about the horse, about Gitanes, not about breathing complaints ... and I would like to hear more about this man called Tom."

"Why don't you drink your tea first?"

For the very life of her Valerie would not touch the cup. "I'm very impatient."

"Without patience you will find out nothing about Gitanes or Tom."

Another sentence like that and she would go for Evi's throat. "I don't think you can imagine how I ..."

"How you feel? Well, how do you feel?"

Valerie took a deep breath.

"How do you feel?" Evi said again.

"To be honest, I haven't come to ... to talk to you about my feelings. I would like to make an agreement with you about the horse. Tell me what you charge per hour, per day, per week. For me to spend time with Gitanes with you present. And for you answering my questions about the horse—because I haven't a clue about horses. Does that sound feasible to you?"

Evi tilted her head to one side, not in thought but rather to fathom what Valerie was planning.

"Last night you dreamt about somebody who suffers from asthma," she said. "That's why I advise you to drink the tea."

"How can you know that?"

"Do you know anybody with asthma?" Evi asked.

"Asthma? ... No, I don't know anybody ..."

"You and this woman are on a large white ship. You are the only passengers."

"It was blue," said Valerie trying to find out whether she could unsettle Evi, but Evi did not react.

She continued instead in a voice as if describing a picture on a cinema screen: "The ship is very large. Be prepared for a fairly long journey. And your only companion is a woman with asthma."

Suddenly Valerie found herself thinking of Mrs Barzi, the woman she had met at the baker's who did actually have asthma. Evi drew her shawl tighter around her shoulders. When Valerie looked at Evi's feet, she saw that she was wearing sandals and coloured socks like a child.

Madness, thought Valerie, the only person who can help me is wearing striped socks. She suddenly felt a waft of affection for Evi Schaefer and yet at the same time she was as crazy as a balloon.

"I would like to see Gitanes," said Valerie.

The ground was soft from the snow which had melted the night before. Evi exchanged her sandals for rubber boots and also offered Valerie a sturdy pair. Together they stomped through the mud. When Gitanes saw them approaching he withdrew to the furthermost corner.

"Would you fetch the horse for me, please?"

"That's impossible," Evi answered.

"But it is running away."

"He is faster than me," Evi said.

"Is he running away from me? But I haven't done anything to him."

"Have you already had enough?"

"No, no!" Valerie answered, indignant. She was frustrated. Why did everything have to be so difficult? She couldn't go either backwards or forwards, she simply stood there, staring at the horse running away.

"Why has this horse entered my life so mysteriously? Why did I find the postcard?—And now, when I try to approach it, it runs away. That makes no sense at all." Gitanes must have heard her sigh because he turned his head and looked over to her, curious. Valerie felt her heart yield. You good horse, you, she thought, and dared to take a few steps towards him—until he ran off again.

"I was too quick," she said. "I've always been too quick."

"No, you were too slow."

"Too slow?"

"You were too slow stopping."

"But how could I have known that? It happened too fast."

"With horses you have to watch very closely."

Again Valerie lost patience. She wanted to go home—no, not home—she wanted to be with the horse, close to it, she wanted to smell it and ... touch it. Not the horse actually but

Miriam, who in her imagination was one with the horse.

"I feel dreadful. Please, help me. Tell me what I should do." It occurred to Valerie that she hadn't given Evi Schaefer a single cent for her service yet. At their last encounter she had been so much beside herself that she had forgotten to. She drew a hundred-Euro-note from her jeans pocket. "Please, take it. I'm sorry, you are sacrificing your time and I'm being ungrateful."

Evi took the note and slipped it into her jacket pocket. Gitanes was watching them again, attentively. What was going through his mind? Valerie risked taking a few more steps and when she saw him put his ears back, she stopped.

"Ears back means annoyance, doesn't it?" said Valerie. This time he didn't run away but stood still, curious.

"Wow," Valerie said and sighed. "I am happy—a horse has actually stopped for me!"

In all the terrible and confusing things that had happened in recent weeks, this seemed to be the first moment she had felt happiness. But it did not last. Immediately her thoughts once again got caught up in an endless spiral of explanations and interpretations.

"Mrs Rosenstein?" she heard Evi say, and awoke from her trance. The horse had started to nibble at the sparse stalks of grass.

"Yes," Valerie replied. "I don't know whether I'll be able to go through with it. I imagined it all differently. I don't think I have any talent with horses."

Gitanes had lost all interest in both Valerie and Evi, and when he saw a horse and rider go by in the distance, he galloped to the fence and whinnied mightily.

"I'm an intelligent woman. I've studied philosophy, my sister even calls me *the superbrain*. But I'm afraid that a superbrain is incapable of making contact with something as animalistic as a horse. I simply think too much, I think practically all the time, even when I'm dreaming. Can you understand that, Mrs Schaefer?"

Evi once again had this hostile expression like an animal just about to bite. "Intelligent people have lots of excuses," she said. "You'd better go home."

"No!" Blossom, the brown horse that had appeared at the window last time, had shown up again and had flinched when Valerie suddenly became so loud. Valerie felt that Gitanes had sent the brown horse because it was too much for him to bother about a miserable creature like her, Valerie Rosenstein. Blossom looked at her as if she was about to collapse under the weight of Valerie's misery. Suddenly she knew what she had to do.

The mud squelched under her boots.

"It's absurd to read any kind of secrets into this horse even if the chain of apparent coincidences around his name is impressive. I can't bear even more humiliation." With that Valerie set off back to the house where she would grab her handbag and disappear in thin air. Evi marched along beside her.

"Who do you think is humiliating you?"

"Nobody. I'm not blaming anybody. I take full responsibility for everything. It's me who leaps at innocent creatures and drives them away and tortures their very soul. From now on I will leave you and your horses in peace. That's the best thing for all of us. By the way, I'm really grateful to you for helping me to become aware of this— and I mean that quite seriously."

Valerie's testimony did not appease Evi Schaefer at all. On the contrary.

She looked at Valerie and said: "Bullshit."

"Really? You're the ruler of the universe, are you? Bullshit, eh! Why don't you fetch your broomstick and fly off to the coven? It was probably you with your supernatural powers, who sent me the asthma dream. You put the post-card in Miriam's locker and came in *by chance* while I was clearing it out. You thought I'd fall for that so easily, but I won't."

Valerie took one last look at the horses and noticed that Gitanes had come closer again. She had to laugh suddenly because the animals' curiosity seemed so amusing. Gitanes scraped the ground with his hoof. Then he went to Blossom and laid his head on her neck. Because Blossom was taller, Gitanes had to stretch his head up—and his eyes rolled as if it was pure bliss for him. He rubbed his chin on the brown horse's mane and peered over at Valerie as if to check that she was watching.

Valerie put her hands in her pockets, forgetting everything and watched the horses. This rubbing became too much for Blossom and she snapped at Gitanes. Gitanes gave her a gentle kick with his hind hooves and came running to Valerie. Valerie's heart was pounding—Does he mean me? Gitanes came to a standstill a few paces away from her.

Although he came very close and although she was usually scared to death of horses, she remained quite calm. He swung his head back and forth and shook himself as if he wanted to get rid of something onerous. Gitanes was not very tall but as he stood before her now, his presence was most impressive. He emanated superior pride, she felt strangely insignificant, he on the other hand seemed to possess sublimity as if it was his birthright. Valerie was amazed by her own thoughts. At the same time she felt somewhat light headed and surrendered to the horse's apparently unshakeable well-being.

Gitanes stretched his head forwards and touched her breast with his muzzle. With his warm breath he breathed into her as if he wanted to reignite extinguished fire. Valerie was weeping.

6

The next few days Valerie was spared further inexplicable coincidences, signs or dreams, and she breathed a sigh of relief. The new year proceeded, it snowed and thawed and snowed and thawed. Valerie made it a habit to visit Gitanes in his field and spend time with him, simply be with him. After a view visits she even felt confident enough to do so without Evi. She returned to her work. She wrote articles for specialist journals, advised authors on non-fiction projects and did editorial work. She dedicated herself to her regular customers and congratulated herself on her occupational independence.

"Rosenstein," Valerie growled into the telephone. "Warmschneider."

That's bad, thought Valerie, Mrs Warmschneider doesn't pay her bills.

"My husband moved out yesterday," the client began.

Valerie tried to apply the brakes: "Our meeting is not until the day after tomorrow."

"It takes all my strength," continued Mrs Warmschneider, "to make this phone call at all. I have to submit the manuscript on Wednesday and I still have to write the last two chapters."

"I've been waiting for them for weeks," Valerie snapped, using a tone she normally didn't apply with clients.

"I wanted to ask you ... can't you write the last two chapters for me. You know the content and you could ... I know you can imitate my style ... you are my last chance."

"Mrs Warmschneider, you have outstanding bills to the extent of 1500 Euro."

"I'll pay everything when I get the advance on the book. I only have to deliver the manuscript."

A raven sitting on the window sill was looking at Valerie with his black pin-head eyes. Just as she had observed Gitanes' expression and behaviour in the last few days, she now tried to interpret the raven's expression. Animals had their special ways. Damn it, the raven looked as all animals do when they want to off-load something.

"To write and edit two chapters in two days is even much for me."

"You could do it if you wanted to." Mrs Warmschneider's tone sounded provocative.

Who wanted what from whom? Valerie noticed that she had started communicating silently with the raven. I make an effort to be friendly with my customers and Mrs Warmschneider is taking shameless advantage of that, Valerie thought.

Mrs Warmschneider started to cry. She told her about her separation, about her money problems and ... Valerie was moved, but not for very long. The raven began to peck about on the window sill. Valerie remembered that a few days before she had shaken breadcrumbs off a tablecloth onto it, but surely they must have long been gobbled up.

The raven looked at her as if he were waiting for her finally to tune into his frequency. Mrs Warmschneider is lying, Valerie thought, feeling that this thought had come to her via the raven. The raven stopped pecking and looked at her expectantly.

Valerie heard herself say to the client: "Your husband

has not left you, Mrs Warmschneider, and I get the feeling that you are trying to manipulate me because you know that I have a soft heart." Silence.

"How do you know that ...?"

Valerie was wondering that herself. "Is it true?"

"I'm glad you have seen through me," the lady replied.

Mrs Warmschneider confessed that she was a notorious liar. She was married to a well-to-do husband, had made a name for herself as a writer of books on healthy eating, but was bored to death. She got a special kick out of telling people stories and testing how credible she was.

"Perhaps you should write novels instead of books on dietetics," Valerie said.

"Why didn't I think of that. This advice is worth its weight in gold, Mrs Rosenstein. Do you really believe I could do that?"

"Absolutely. I'm quite sure you could."

The raven flew off. Valerie grinned as if a whole basket of butterflies was dancing in her stomach.

Three days later 2500 Euro landed on her account with the note: "for your clairvoyance."

Valerie smiled at the raven who was perched in the cherry tree and she said: "You're really good."

"There is someone here who would like to meet you," shouted Evi across the field to Valerie, who was just feeding the horses. "Are you prepared for that?"

"For what?" asked Valerie in response, and momentarily allowed herself to be distracted. Gitanes tore the bucket of horse food out of her hand and the muesli was scattered in the mud. Annoyed, Valerie ran over to the house to fetch some more.

"You've spilled his muesli," Evi grumbled.

"Who wants to speak to me?"

"I'll send him away. It's not the right moment."

Valerie heaved a deep sigh. "Who?"

"This encounter will change your life."

Could she tone it down a bit? Evi had the annoying habit of exaggerating. The wind surged through the bare trees and bushes and the last snow slid off the roof. Then the sun came out and Valerie squinted. She heard her heart racing. Perhaps Evi had really meant that thing about changing her life. She turned to Gitanes. He looked at her with large, dark eyes. A sentence popped into Valerie's head which seemed to come from Gitanes: You don't need to be afraid, we are in this game together. She turned and found herself looking into the eyes of a half-breed Indian.

He was standing on the terrace. His black hair reached to his shoulders, his nose was broad, his lips dark brown and his eyes reminded Valerie of the werewolf on the film poster hanging on the barn door where you entered the village of Schlattstall.

"My name is Tom. I'm pleased to meet you." He spoke German with an American accent. The invisible energy which he emanated virtually bowled Valerie over.

"Why have you come?" she asked in a faltering voice.

He did not answer, but appeared instead to suck up her energy as animals did. And then she knew the answer: because of me.

Gitanes came running up to Tom as if to an old friend he hadn't seen for a long time. He laid his head on Tom's shoulder as if it was his TV armchair. Valerie looked away because it seemed so intimate to her. She heard Tom talking to the horse in some foreign language.

She felt envious and disappointed because she had thought that Gitanes belonged to her and that there was nothing more important than the sworn union that had developed in recent weeks, which of course was totally far-fetched.

"I am Valerie and I'm pleased to meet you, too."

Valerie would have liked to unpack her tape recorder and microphone and ask Tom endless questions ... Who was he? Why was he in Germany? Was he taking part in the Indian rituals which involved pushing meat hooks through their skin? Why, according to Evi, had he brought Gitanes here three months before Miriam's death—as a *medicine horse*?

As she looked at Tom, she knew that all these questions were ridiculous and that Tom had a secret which made all the questions superfluous. And she, Valerie Rosenstein, would have given anything to discover this secret.

7

Miou was whining pitifully because Valerie sat glued to the sofa instead of finally serving her her salmon pâté. Valerie had just had a phone call from her sister, Tamara, who had sounded pretty disturbed, was almost crying. Miou curled herself round Valerie's ankles like a charmed snake.

"I can't believe Tamara has actually persuaded me to meet her," Valerie said to Miou. "She only wants to finish me off, somehow that's what everyone is trying to do: Evi, Mrs Warmschneider … and probably everybody else has always done that, too, only I had never noticed. Except you, of course." "Eeeaaaooouuu," answered Miou and Valerie set off to the cat-food cupboard.

And Tom—he also found it repugnant to use other people, or take advantage of them. Several times she had met him at Evi's and to some extent they had become friends, even if in this case 'friendship' was not quite the right word. Tom lived according to a different time scale and clearly did not inhabit the orderly, reasonable universe that Valerie called home. She still knew virtually nothing about him because he often remained silent. But Valerie loved Tom's silence. He was the first man with whom she was not totally overwhelmed by despair about the impossibility of man and woman ever putting up with one another on the same planet.

Valerie would've liked to have had somebody she could have talked to about Tom and her confusing feelings and thoughts, but Tamara would only turn it into second-rate, tastelessly soppy schmaltz and that was certainly not what was happening between her and Tom. Not the slightest trace of a concocted love story.

Tamara submitted to being dragged forward by her hooligan of a boxer. The February wind blew icy cold, the accumulated frustration of a winter trying to prove to all and sundry that it was not done for yet.

Valerie started the conversation by saying: "You wanted to talk to me about something."

Tamara jerked the boxer back by his collar, which only led to him flapping about like a hooked fish being hauled in.

"There are a few weird things happening with Mark. ... I'm almost ashamed to tell you about them ..." Tamara said.

Not surprised, thought Valerie. I can well imagine it. Nothing good can come from that mean bastard.

"It's not fair to blubber it all out to you," Tamara continued, "with you having just lost your daughter. You have much bigger problems."

"Why did you ask to talk to me then?" Valerie asked soberly.

"Because you, Super Brain, don't react so ... emotionally to things ...." Tamara smiled conspiratorially.

Thanks for the compliment, Valerie thought, and nodded.

"You think before you feel," Tamara continued.

Tamara had always separated their roles into: Miss Emotional and Super Brain.

"Has Mark got a mistress?" Valerie asked with deliberate neutrality.

"Something has gone wrong with him emotionally. As if he had suffered some trauma," Tamara said.

There is nothing new about that, thought Valerie, it's just that Tamara had never noticed before. Valerie suddenly realized that Tamara's walk was conspicuously lopsided.

"You've got pains in your legs," Valerie said.

"Yes, Valerie, I fell over."

"You fell?" Valerie wanted to say: I thought Mark had beaten you up, but she checked herself. The time wasn't ripe for that. Valerie heard Gitanes say: All information at the right time. "Sorry to hear that. When did it happen?"

"Three days ago."

"You wanted to tell me something about Mark."

"His firm is facing a crisis. They've put him on short time. That has dented his ego. Things are great for me, they have enlarged my department and I'm earning more." Tamara elaborated by explaining to Valerie how superb she was at scanning her fellow workers. Yet her scanning abilities seemed to have failed with Mark. "The best thing would be for me to resign from my job and stop working for a while. We've got enough saved. Just till Mark gets back on his feet."

Madness. Tamara allowed Mark to be beat her up and yet she wanted to sacrifice her job just to protect his wilting ego. "Do you really think that's the way to improve things?" Valerie asked with deliberate innocence.

"Mark needs it. He's an alpha animal." The boxer ran ahead at full tilt and dragged Tamara limping after him. Valerie felt a surge of sympathy, or was it helplessness? She couldn't tell which.

The path went along a canal and suddenly Valerie stopped involuntarily. Over a stone wall she glimpsed the dull water rippling in the wind. The trees and bushes on the bank were still grey with winter but there was something in the air: a delicate fragrance of spring, which was still too faint for the human nose to detect. But a horse could smell it, Valerie thought, and lifted her nose to inhale more of it.

Things will get even worse between Tamara and Mark, Valerie thought and felt very sad.

A freighter barge as long and thin as an eel slid past, with nobody on deck, it seemed like a ghost ship. Like the ship in my dream, thought Valerie, and it didn't have a captain either.

She noticed that meanwhile Tamara and the dog had got way ahead and she set off to catch them up. Valerie was pretty much out of breath when she reached Tamara, but the boxer still had plenty of energy. A black-and-white border collie appeared and Tamara's dog, with the impressive name of Alexander, tugged even more wildly at the lead.

"Tell me what to do!" shouted Tamara in despair.

Valerie meant to suppress her answer but this time the right moment for the right information had come: "Kick Mark in the backside and then get the hell out as fast as you can," Valerie said.

Tamara's expression froze, then she brightened up. "Then you do have feelings!"

8

"Hard to believe I'm sitting on a horse. It feels like ... as if I were sitting in a UFO, I'm floating. No, sorry, it's just so incredible. I've always been so extremely afraid of horses and ... well, you know what happened to my daughter and ..." Tom was walking along beside Valerie and did not say a word. Gitanes did not seem to be bothered by Valerie sitting on his back either.

"So sorry to be talking so much but it's such an unusual experience for me." Valerie pushed aside a branch that was just about to whip her in the face. She wondered what was more unusual: exchanging messages with ravens and horses—or actually riding a horse.

Only a saddle pad separated her from Gitanes' back, she could feel the moist warmth of his body, the undulating power of his muscles. It was one thing to be walking on the ground next to a horse, turtle-doving head to head with it, and another to be growing from the centre of its body and moving forwards on four legs rather than two. There were no words to express this weird feeling.

Tom was walking beside Valerie, striding evenly.

Here and there spring was beginning to show its first virginal green, everywhere the imminent green explosion could now be clearly felt and likewise: the first enchanted sunbeams soaked with warmth. Ahead of them their path was crossed by another, which led deeper into the forest.

"There's something I'd like to talk to you about," Tom said and his voice sounded darker and more mysterious than usual. "Are you ready?"

"Yes." Silently she added: of course, I'm burning up with curiosity. At the same time a slight trembling awoke in the depths of her body which increased inexorably and developed into a shuddering earthquake. What would Tom dish up once he spoke instead of remaining mysteriously silent? She felt Gitanes likewise becoming slightly nervous, no wonder when you're carrying around a small earthquake on your back. When they reached the crossing, Tom halted the horse.

"Which way do you want to go? It's your decision." There was something urgent in his words but perhaps it just seemed that way to her. The situation was symbolic. They were standing at a crossing of the ways. Tom was obviously being drawn left into the forest—but when she looked that way the threatening feeling became stronger as if some reptile were lurking there just waiting to devour her. To the right along a field there stretched a boring tarmac road.

"I'm a bit frightened," she said.

"What of?"

"Of the forest, of what is awaiting me."

Tom nodded. "What would you like to do?"

"My reason would like to know what exactly will happen there in the forest and how it'll turn out. Then it would be ready to agree." Valerie laughed. "Of course I know there's no insurance policy where secrets are concerned but ... it still gives me the creeps."

"The *creeps*," said Tom laughing, too, he apparently liked the word.

Gitanes started to shift from one foot to the other. This standing waiting and her indecisiveness were simply taking too long.

"Can't we let Gitanes decide?" Valerie said and was almost proud of her idea.

Tom slung the lead rope round the horse's neck and knotted it tight. "No, I didn't mean you to take that seriously. Help, I'm sitting on a horse and there is no way I can control it. What if he suddenly runs off? Then I'm lost (lost! lost! lost!)". But Gitanes simply made a turn and went back to a patch of juicy green grass that they had just passed and began to eat. Valerie was disappointed. Inwardly she had already decided on the adventure in the forest and had imagined that Gitanes, in a heroic gesture, would agree with her and march off into the forest full of vigour.

"It's my own fault. That's what I get for indecisiveness. I want to go into the forest!" said Valerie.

Tom seized the lead rope and led Gitanes back to the crossing and then straight into the promising secrecy. Valerie suspected that she had followed neither her own nor Gitanes' wish, but that Tom had subtly fixed the whole thing. I was asking for it, she thought.

The light fell in repeatedly new angles through the thicket and onto mossy stones which shimmered like dark velvet. She smelled damp earth, decay and sweet wood and the rustling of the leaves induced a faint trance. Perhaps today I'll find out what the whole thing with Tom and Gitanes is all about, thought Valerie, why they have come into my life.

Out of the darkness there unfolded a clearing like a cathedral of light stretching to the clouds. Valerie's fear vanished before this impressive sight and she took a deep breath, taking in the moist, fresh forest air.

"This is a wonderful place," she said. "It has unusual energy." Gitanes nibbled at the leaves within reach of his outstretched neck.

"Let's go a bit further." Tom seemed to be looking for a

particular place. Pine woods stretched beyond the clearing, the atmosphere here was darker, the light only penetrated into the brush in a few places, which had the effect of a mouldering dungeon. The tree trunks were so close together that you could hardly even penetrate on foot, let alone on a horse.

Valerie was freezing inside and out.

Tom drew the horse up and only now did Valerie realize that here the tree trunks took on an almost circular formation, in the centre of which there was a round, open area.

Valerie slid off the horse's back. It was totally silent in this part of the forest, no animals seemed to venture here, perhaps because the trees seemed to have been planted in orderly ranks and the place exuded an aura of lifelessness and threat.

Tom tied Gitanes to a branch, then lifted his leather bag over his head and laid it down on a bed of pine needles. He flipped open the flap of the bag and pulled out a linen cloth. It bore a simple drawing which Valerie could not immediately decipher.

Tom strewed a handful of earth in all four directions, bowed and squatted down. It was cold, they were wearing anoraks, gloves and woollen hats. Valerie felt even colder, now that the horse no longer warmed her. Gitanes stood there with his head bowed reverently as if he, too, was expecting something mysterious.

Then Tom began to sing, sounds full of vowels and consonants as hard as polished stones. Valerie studied the drawing on the unfurled cloth. It showed a long ship, curved up at stem and stern, and now she also realized that the scrawled marks represented people travelling on the ship. What came to mind was the dream she had had on the walk with her sister: the asthmatic woman and the white ship and the ghostly barge.

Suddenly she had the feeling that there was somebody here to her right. *She* is here, thought Valerie. While she was trying to fathom the presence of this being more fully Valerie heard Tom's singing change to an asthmatic rattling, as if he, too, felt the presence of a ghost. Surely he did.

"Who are you?" asked Valerie, but received no answer. She had the feeling that the ghost wanted to reveal itself but that something was preventing that. She was fairly sure that it was Miriam who had appeared, she had read in several books that people who had been violently snatched from life, remained trapped in the earthly world or in an intermediate world. And had her stupid sister not said something similar about Miriam still being here? Valerie's whole body was vibrating. What should she do now? What does one do in such a situation? Surely anyone as unfamiliar with ghosts as she was, would only get it all wrong. She could ask Tom, but she would only make a total fool of herself and disturb his concentration. Furthermore such banal questions would drive away the ghost immediately. Valerie hardly dared to breathe now. The main thing was that the ghost should stay there until she had sorted herself out. When would she ever have such an opportunity again?

Valerie surrendered to Tom's singing and allowed herself to drift along with whatever was to happen. She still clearly felt the ghost's presence, noticed how her gaze repeatedly wandered back to the drawing and suddenly she had the distinct feeling that the ghost was one of the figures on the ship. She was struck by a deep feeling of disquiet, as if she were witnessing a terrifying occurrence. She saw red hair. Mrs Barzi, the neighbour with the dyed-red hair, who had pressed the book into her hands in the baker's shop, the one who rattled when she breathed. Now Valerie remembered the title of the book: *"Conversations With the Dead."*

She felt freezing cold. "She is on this ship," Valerie said in a quivering voice. "She is going over." Gitanes was chewing and licking extensively.

"Why are we here?" she blurted out. Tom, squatting opposite her, lifted his head and their eyes met. Never before had she looked so deeply into his eyes. His gaze was soft and she seemed to be looking through some opening, directly into the heart of a truly benevolent soul.

"You summoned me," said Tom. "Don't you remember?"

"Me? No! When can that have been?"

"Nearly nine months ago."

Valerie worked it out. That must have been in the summer when Miriam was still alive. She had the accident in September. Valerie could not remember anything specific.

"How did I summon you?"

"You asked for support. So I sent you Gitanes."

"I don't remember."

"At that time you were not yet listening to your soul."

Feverishly Valerie tried to remember.

"Does that mean my soul knew, or guessed, that my daughter would die?"

"The soul knows many things."

"If I had known that, I would have done anything to prevent it," said Valerie and was overwhelmed by pain and despair. "What are we doing here? What does this ship mean? ... They are dead, aren't they, those people travelling on the ship ... over to the Realm of the Dead?" Valerie could hardly express the words. "Just now I had the feeling that Mrs Barzi, a neighbour of mine, is on that ship. I saw her in a dream, we were together on a ship ... What does it all mean? I want an explanation—right now!"

"I've brought you here because ..." Tom paused as if what he had to say was utterly inexpressible.

"Tell me, please."

"You must not think that *I* have invoked all this. I'm just the messenger."

"I don't understand. Whose messenger?"

"You'll find out."

"I want to know now."

"I cannot tell you. I have come here because I have been sent."

"Who...?"

Tom remained silent.

Gitanes became restless. He jerked his head back and forth. "I don't understand any of this," said Valerie. The horse began to tug at the rope as if he wanted to tear himself free. Valerie was afraid he might injure himself if he continued to react so violently.

Tom stood up and untied the quick-release knot in the lead rope.

Gitanes was finally free. He ran up to the cloth on the ground, stopped and lowered his head. All at once an almost ethereal calm emanated from him. Then he shook his head, three times, slowly and deliberately, then he paused. He stood still for a moment, then he shook his head again, tossing his mane to the opposite side of his head.

"Why is he doing that?" Valerie asked. "What does it mean?"

Again the horse shook his head. His forelock flew to and fro. A hot-and-cold tremour gripped Valerie. That's just how Miriam shook her head. Exactly the same movement, the same expression. Her blonde fringe had always flown back and forth just like that.

"Miriam!" shrieked Valerie horrified. She burst into tears, and, unable to stand any longer, sank to her knees.

It now occurred to her that once that last summer Miriam had talked about death. Valerie had thought that those were normal thoughts for a girl her age. They were standing by a horses' field and Miriam had said: "If I die, I will be in the horses' paradise. Like the gypsies." Recently a gypsy family had bought a house on the edge of the village and Miriam had made friends with one of the children, a girl called Maria. *Gitanes* was French for gypsy. Had Miriam had a premonition of her death? But how was that possible? Valerie had the feeling that a gust of wind was sweeping through her feather-like thoughts so that they fluttered about then resettled in a different order with some enigmatic significance. Since Miriam's death everything in her life had become chaotic. Valerie suspected that she would never really be able to fully fathom that.

She looked at Tom and for a long time rested in his calm gaze which seemed to her like home. "I have understood a little bit of it," she said. "And this tiny bit is already gigantic, it is ... I can't find any words for it but perhaps I don't need them after all." Tom smiled wisely, as was his way. Then Valerie felt the ghost evaporating and the place where she found herself changed back from a twilight world between life and death into a dark forest. She had a feeling of inner peace.

Tom thanked the spirits who had come. He bowed to all four winds, scattering a handful of earth each time then rolled the cloth up again.

Valerie hooked the lead rope on again, while Gitanes stood there calmly and content. She stroked his neck.

"Thank you, my medicine horse," she said.

She made her way back on foot. It felt good to walk together in silence through the green darkness, shot through with smells and light—in silence but intimately connected in some light and independent way. So much happiness, thought Valerie, and felt the frozen grief about Miriam's death beginning to melt a little.

9

On her way home Valerie stopped in front of Mrs Barzi's house, in the road that led to the "Golden Hole", a rock cave in which, according to legend, golden treasure lay hidden. She rang the doorbell but the occupant was not there. Valerie stopped at the baker's, bought a loaf and, unable to restrain herself said: "I rang Mrs Barzi's bell, I wanted to give her back a book she'd lent me. Do you know ...?"

Tightening her lips the shop-assistant, Mrs Mohnhaupt, who had been selling bread here for thirty years and knew all about everything living or dead in the village, said: "Mrs Barzi died last night. 'N asthma attack, she'd 'ad it a long time. She were a nice woman."

Valerie was in tears as she took the bag with the loaf in it. "Yes, she was a perceptive woman. So, I suppose I'll have to keep the book. Tell me, do you know when the funeral is?"

"Wensdy at two in't woodland cemetery. S'pose yer knew her better'n me."

"Yes, she gave me something very precious."

The assistant smiled at Valerie meaningfully.

"T'were pretty bad 'er asthma. Now she be free of 'er misery. She were a nice woman."

That evening Valerie phoned Tom and invited him to join her for breakfast. She wanted to tell him about Mrs Barzi, the woman on the ship. The morning, thought Valerie, was a perfectly harmless time, when the spirits were at rest— and she had examined herself and her motives carefully beforehand. She liked Tom, that was all. No love story, Tom was now a part of her life and she had finally learned to accept the invitations which recently life had unmistakably been delivering to her. Tom said: "Delighted to come."

From the cellar Valerie fetched the honey she had bought from Hans, the bee keeper, who had his hives at the edge of the village. It was a dark honey, as dark as the forests, which spread across the slopes all around Schlattstall.

While she was laying the breakfast table she thought once more about her last encounter with Mrs Barzi at the baker's. She took the book from the shelf and ran her hand over the cover. Then she lit a candle. "Thank you," she said. "For everything. And have a good crossing." Suddenly tears began to flow. "Miriam will be there. She's an angel. Take her my greetings."

The doorbell rang. As Tom came in, the atmosphere changed, he brought a lightness into the room and a joy-ousness that was not expressed in grand gestures, it could be felt rather than seen.

"I like this village," said Tom as he spread honey on a slice of the oven-baked bread. "It has steep slopes on three sides."

"Many people find it gloomy." Valerie said. "But I like it, too. I feel rather as if I were in a cradle here … Find your way alright?"

Tom nodded. Miou had discovered the newcomer and was rubbing herself against his legs. She mewed at him as he stroked her with those large hands of his, they were so gentle that Valerie was almost shocked. She had noticed before the softness and gentleness of his gestures when she had seen him with Gitanes. It was women who were thought to be the soft and gentle ones, but this man was far gentler than she was, she thought. Is that why he could handle animals so well?

"How do you come to know Evi?" Valerie asked. It was the first time that they had met anywhere other than at Evi's.

"She did her training with a friend of mine."

"Her training as a shamanic healer? Where was that? In Germany or the States? Does he have a website?" Valerie bit her lip because she noticed the journalist in her gaining the upper hand.

As was to be expected, Tom did not answer.

That business with information. In Valerie's world you asked questions and got answers. In Tom and Evi's world the information came at the right time, in the right place, *from* the right person *to* the right person, and you could do nothing to accelerate this.

Miou jumped onto Tom's lap. She seemed to have fallen for him. With infinite patience he jerked the plastic mouse, she had brought him, up and down while she spun in circles on her own axis.

After a while Tom said, "She is very fond of you." Then he went straight on: "I'll be flying to the States next week. Come with me if you want to."

Valerie had the feeling someone had struck a huge golden gong and its sound set the walls of her house vibrating. Her mind tried to grasp what he had just said. Their eyes met and again she felt that calmness and security, and also attraction. As if he had put an arm round her and said: 'Come with me. It'll work out.' But Valerie could not simply accept it just like that. Her thoughts ran wild. Which Valerie did he mean? Valerie, his horse's friend? Valerie, an acquaintance of his friend Evi? Valerie, the woman ...? She had met him a few times at Evi's, exchanged a few sentences with him, and they had had this impressive experience together in the forest. Something inexplicable, something mystical had brought Tom into her life. He belonged in her life like an old acquaintance yet at the same time he was a stranger.

"Excuse me, Tom." Valerie felt a strong urge to go outside. She opened the terrace door and stepped out into the garden. The crocuses were in bloom, orange-yellow and violet, snowdrops formed a field of white dots under the plum tree. A handful of forlorn, fleecy clouds drifted dreamily across the bright-blue sky. A tractor droned in the distance. The shadow of the garden fence stretched almost up to Valerie's feet.

It was not easy to imagine many days spent in Tom's presence, with this combination of calmness and energy which exuded from him, powerful and overwhelming not because he intended it but because she had nothing to resist him with. That's another reason why she didn't understand why he had invited her to join him on this journey. How could he find someone like her interesting? And anyway, she couldn't just simply disappear to America. Where do we think we are? And who are we anyway? Why was he doing this—for her?

Valerie cast a fleeting glance back into the house and saw Tom sitting alone at the dining table. He didn't belong there, he looked as if he was from an alien planet, stranded. But it did not seem to bother him.

If I ask him why he is inviting me, he will probably say he is just the messenger. I really would like to get to know someone like him better, but to go on a journey with a total stranger? To such a far-off country? Valerie took a deep breath and went back in. She was simply *in* this situation and had to act.

"I know this is a bit difficult for you," Tom said. Valerie took a sip of coffee and noticed it had gone cold. She must have been in the garden for quite a long time.

"Would you like another coffee? Or something else? Tea perhaps?"

"The coffee was very good, I would very much like another," Tom said.

Valerie put the kettle on.

"How long have you been in Germany?" she asked a bit later, holding the handle of the warm coffee pot in one hand and curling her other hand around it.

"I came twenty years ago with the army."

"Are you still in the army?"

"No, haven't been for a long time."

"Why did you stay here?"

He shook his head and with a silvery laugh said: "Because of the horses."

"Haven't you got enough horses over there? You've got far more room for them."

"It was because of a particular horse. Gitanes' father. I brought him to Germany from Morocco because he asked me to do that for him." Tom's features, which were already smooth and hardly showed any signs of age, relaxed even slightly more. His whole body seemed to surrender to an image which he found very pleasant and this gave her an impression of how much Tom's life was linked with horses.

"What was the horse's name?"

"Jacques-le-mérite."

"Jacques-deserves-it?" Valerie translated the French name literally.

Tom smiled. "Yes, and his name did suit him. He did deserve ... to have a good life. He repaid my efforts a thousand-fold."

"Is he still alive?"

"He died—last year."

"When?"

"September 23rd."

"That's not true!" Valerie's throat seized up. "On the same day as Miriam!" Valerie put the coffee pot down on the table. The morning sun was shining onto the wooden floor now, bathing the sofa, the carved feet of the old cupboard and the wrought-iron stove in a dazzling light.

"Would you come with me to Miriam's room?" Valerie asked. She felt the need to show Tom the room. Again she had the feeling that the curtain covering a mysterious reality, behind which unfathomable threads were woven, had briefly opened. Furthermore, for the first time since Miriam had been born, she had the feeling she had gained access to that aspect of Miriam that had always frightened and alienated her somewhat. Because Miriam und Tom had many things in common, even if this was not obvious at first glance. Miriam, too, had had this calm radiance and this intuitive knowledge about hidden things.

The room consisted of a bunk bed under which stood a two-seater sofa, opposite a desk and a chair. The walls were covered with horse posters, the shelves filled with toy horses. Miriam had also painted horses: standing under a rainbow, in a garden paradise, horses with wings and without wings, in all colours, shapes and sizes. Valerie opened a drawer and pulled out a stack of drawings, done with coloured crayons and chalk. She handed Tom a drawing of a girl with blonde hair standing beside a paint horse.

"This is Miriam?" said Tom.

Valerie nodded, tears filled her eyes. "And that is Jacques, isn't it?"

"Yes," said Tom.

Valerie turned the drawing over. On the back it read in large letters: JACQUES.

"She was no ordinary girl," Tom said.

"No." Tears were now spilling from Valerie's eyes, she

was sobbing and for a long time she could not utter a single word.

"She had special abilities ... but I never took them seriously, ... many people thought that there was something not quite right about her! And I feel eternally sorry that I, as her mother, did not stand fully behind her. I simply cannot forgive myself for that. I didn't know enough about these things. In school she was often somewhere else, her teachers said ... she had to repeat a year. She had no real friends, she talked very little, she couldn't bear crowds, five people in a room were already too much for her. My family considered her ill-mannered and unfriendly." Valerie was overwhelmed by the need to talk about Miriam. "I loved her just as she was, but there was something in me that believed she had to adjust to survive in this world. I believed I had to change her, to educate her. I tortured her with that and she was probably often desperate. ... I made an enormous mistake." Valerie was trembling all over and the tears ran down her cheeks. She sat down on the chair at the desk and saw the raven sitting on the window sill. Shyly she waved to him and wiped away her tears.

"I'm sorry for inundating you with my feelings like this," she said to Tom.

Tom went and stood by the window and looked out. Valerie put the drawing back in the drawer. Suddenly she was suffused with great calm and her hesitancy about whether to fly to the USA with Tom dissolved.

"I think Miriam would want me to join you on this journey," she said.

Valerie disappeared to the toilet and when she came back, she found Tom in the garden. He had sat down on one of the garden chairs, letting the sun bathe his face. Valerie fetched a second chair and sat down next to him.

"Can you tell me something about this trip? Where are

we going exactly and what can we expect there?"

"Lots of questions all at once."

"Sorry. Where are we going?"

"To the state of Arizona."

"For how long?"

"A week."

"And what is waiting for us there?"

"The tribe."

"The tribe?" Valerie tried to visualize something for this word.

"The tribe, who are they? An Indian tribe?"

"You'll see."

Valerie felt that the information Tom was supposed to give her at this point was running low.

"Just one more question," she said. "Why me?"

Tom smiled mysteriously as always. "You are one of us. We have been waiting for you."

10

Her passport was still valid. Valerie opened her appoint-ments diary: she could move the various commissions and engagements without too much of a problem. That just left Miou. Since Tom's visit the cat had stuck to her like glue as if she knew she was going to be left on her own—if only for a week. Valerie did not know anyone in the village well enough to ask them to look after the cat, to be more precise: she did not want to know anybody so well. She valued her anonymity. Her parents had a dog, her sister had a dog. Miou couldn't stand dogs. Her female friends lived a long way away, which for somebody who worked primarily with the computer and the phone was not surprising. Apart from that the number of animal lovers amongst them was not very large, which had to do with the fact that the number of friends she had was already approaching zero.

The flight to Tucson, Arizona, was planned for the Thursday. On Monday morning Miou vomited on the Berber carpet in the bedroom. At lunchtime she vomited on the living room carpet and the kitchen tiles, the rest of the day she lay in the washing basket. In the evening Valerie put Miou in the transport box and drove to Evi's place.

"There's no way I'll take in a sick cat. I'm shocked that you even expect me to." The ever-moody shamanic guide was in a particularly bad mood today.

"I don't expect it, I merely asked."

Evi took a look in the box. "She will really suffer. The very thought that you will leave her alone has already got to her. The message is clear."

"Sorry I asked. I'll find somebody else," Valerie said.

"You mustn't leave her alone," Evi replied and her glance sliced the air in two like a blade.

"That's why I asked you, I know that with you she'll be well looked after." Valerie was determined not to give up so easily.

"I understand Miou, but I don't like your energy. You want to go to Arizona to a meeting of Indian healers. But who are you? A tourist, a spy, a parasite?" Evi said.

Valerie was not quite sure how the relationship between Tom and Evi stood and whether she was perhaps jealous. Had Evi expected Tom to take her, the experienced shaman, with him? Perhaps Evi was even in love with Tom, but that was no concern of hers and she would rather bite off her tongue than ask about it.

Evi disappeared into the kitchen and Valerie followed her. It would have been best to simply go, but Valerie didn't want to accept this treatment.

"What have I done to you?"

"Your energy is very negative," Evi repeated even more malevolently.

"My energy? ... I'm fine."

"You're not sufficiently protected for this experience."

"Then explain to me how I can protect myself."

"I can't convey that to you in one afternoon—and neither do I want to." Evi started to rinse cups and plates. Valerie felt extremely unwanted but she didn't wish to let go. "I can take good care of myself," she replied petulantly.

Evi laughed dismissively. "You know nothing. Your daughter's death has made you vulnerable, you follow every sign, every clue and haven't noticed how many copy cats have established themselves on your ship. You are easy prey for them. They are already rubbing their hands." Evi said it without a trace of malice, as if she really were worried. After all she really was experienced with spirits, death and all those mysterious forms of energy.

Valerie felt this was getting to her. What was Evi trying to say?

"Can you somehow explain that more clearly?"

"You say you can look after yourself," Evi went on. "By that you mean your reason. But your reason cannot protect you."

You're trying to insult my *superbrain*, thought Valerie. Say what you like, my superbrain has never yet let me down. Great, you have made yourself comfortable in your floppy-hat world. But a superbrain can also be quite useful when everything around you starts flying about. All the same the comment about her vulnerability and Miriam's death got to her.

Evi had found her favourite topic: energetic self-protection, the basis of all spiritual work.

"You have no respect for spirits and because you have no respect you have no protection."

"I don't have to protect myself against something I don't know."

"You don't know the spirits but they know you."

"I won't let you scare me," Valerie replied rattily.

"All you care about is experiencing something sensational and writing a book about it afterwards. You haven't the faintest idea what devastating damage you can cause like that. Your cat is showing you but you're not taking it seriously."

Valerie noticed how she was tightening up inwardly. "Let the spirits come, I've got garlic in my luggage."

Evi answered with a dirty laugh. Possibly the spirits'

laughter was equally dirty.

"Is there anything else you'll need to warn me about?"

"I feel really sorry for your cat. She has to bear the brunt."

"It should be possible to leave Miou alone for a week. Let's be down to earth about it, she is a cat."

"That's what I mean. You think you can tear the secrets from the sacred world and let an animal suffer for that. I don't understand why Tom does not see that. Well, he's only a man after all."

That did it. She shouldn't have insulted Tom.

"You are so self-righteous it makes me sick."

"You are leaving your cat in the lurch just as you left Miriam, simply to go chasing your egotistic pleasures."

"What?!!! That's just about enough. How dare you reproach me with leaving Miriam in the lurch?"

"Were you ever in the stable with her? She was always alone with Korbas. You only ever drove up in your Mini to collect her, preferably without even setting foot on the farm. You didn't care a damn about who Miriam really was. You didn't know her. You hadn't the faintest idea."

"If you say another word, I'll wring your neck, you weirdo!" Valerie had never ever talked to anyone like that before but Evi had struck her most vulnerable spot and she couldn't help hitting back brutally.

"Get out of my house!" Evi screeched burning with rage.

"With pleasure!" Valerie replied.

"I want nothing more to do with you."

"That's just what I wanted to say to you. You can kiss my ....!"

Valerie shot like a bolt out of Evi's front door and slammed it so hard behind her that the whole house shook.

How could I have lost control like that, Valerie asked herself. Is it Evi's fault or mine or what's actually going on here?

And where am I going to find a place for Miou now?

11

In Arizona it was—according to *www.accuweather.com* — between 17 and 20 degrees Celsius; in the local bank in Esslingen on the river Neckar they had dollars. Only Miou was still suffering miserably. Valerie recognized Tamara's number on her phone display.

"Hi, how are things?" Tamara's voice sounded extremely gushing. "I have resigned from my job. Isn't that fantastic? Things are great between Mark and me again ... boy, am I glad. And how are you?"

It always gave Valerie stomach ache to hear Tamara talking like this. "I'm flying to the USA for a few days," Valerie said. "And I urgently need someone to look after my cat."

"What are you going to do in the USA?" Tamara drew out the vowels in U-S-A as if they were chewing gum and Valerie noticed how envious her sister was; that's how it had always been even when Valerie had her first three-wheeler bike and when she had her hair done for the graduation ball.

"I'm researching for a book."

"What sort of book?"

"About cactuses."

"Since when have you been interested in cactuses?" Tamara did not wait for the answer but instead enthused about the spin that she and Mark had taken—in his new Porsche—to Ludwig II's castle: Hohenschwangau.

"Couldn't you take Miou for ten days?"

"But I've got Alexander." The boxer.

"You could fix up the guest room for Miou and simply keep the door closed."

Tamara sighed. Down the telephone line Valerie tried to guess the answer before it was expressed, an ability which in recent weeks had considerably improved.

Tamara would—against all odds—say yes.

"OK."

"You can't imagine how relieved I am," Valerie replied—whole-heartedly. "I'll really owe you one."

"For you, sister dear always. You are the only one I can talk openly to, have I ever told you that? All my girlfriends envy me, envy me Mark, the big house, my professional successes. I always have to tone things down. But you are above such things, you don't envy me at all."

Valerie wondered how could anyone envy her Mark. Apparently Tamara had successfully suppressed her problems with Mark because she was still wallowing to some extent in her *I'm-rich-successful-and-to-be-pitied*-lament. Then she declared with the same heavy pathos: "I don't begrudge you your trip one bit. You've had such a hard time—and I'm happy to take your cat. That's the least one can do for one's sister."

That afternoon Miou was better. Whether it had to do with the phone call, or not—perhaps it did, then again: perhaps not. In any case Miou's re-awakened cheerfulness contributed considerably to Valerie gradually starting to look forward to the trip. She sat in her rocking chair, observing the blackbirds, and in her inner eye watched Indians and their horses dancing in a circle. Miou jumped onto her lap. "I've never done anything like this before, Miou, travelling to a foreign country with a man I hardly know and there …

meet my *tribe* who is *waiting* for me." Valerie put down Miou, who complained, and rushed to her computer. She opened a map of Arizona, studied the towns, the geography, the vegetation—and spent half the night reading up the history of the Apache tribe. She printed out a photograph of the silhouette of a mountain chain which, if you examined it carefully, represented a sleeping medicine woman: *Wright Peak.* The right peak, Valerie thought. It'll all work out.

The one sad thing was that Valerie could not say good-bye to Gitanes, because Evi would probably have greeted her with a shotgun. From Miriam's room she collected the postcard with the paint horse, drove to the Breitenstein, her favourite rock formation, and admired the sunset. "Gi-tanes, my friend, my medicine horse, don't let me down, over there, across the pond. I'm counting on you. When I'm up to my neck in water, you'll have to Morse-code me the right messages. And don't forget the time difference, al-right?"

When she looked up into the clouds, it was as if she saw a paint horse hovering past in slow motion.

The blue hold-all stood packed in the hall next to the coat rack, the olive-grey canvas handbag, as well as the blue all-weather anorak, lay on top of it, they would both go as hand luggage. She had dropped Miou off at Tamara's the day be-fore, together with a cardboard box of Miou's favourite food.

Valerie had ordered the taxi for eight o'clock, she was to meet Tom at nine at the Delta Airlines terminal in Stuttgart.

Valerie stood in the garden, with her eyes closed, and concentrated on her breathing. She summoned the spirit of the cherry tree, of the plum tree, the apple tree, the magno-lia, of the raven, the blackbirds, the spirit of Gitanes and any other willing spirits and asked them to stand by her during her flight on the wings of the great iron bird.

As if from a vast distance a sweet, flattering melody reached her ears. The call of a being from the world beyond the great curtain answering her request. After the third repetition Valerie realized that it was the doorbell ringing. "Tamara!" One glance at the transport box in her sister's left hand landed Valerie with a jolt back on the hard ground of facts. The interweave of fate. Tamara's mascara was smudged, her eye blackened."

"I can't take Miou or Mark will kill me."

"My flight leaves in three hours. What can I do?"

"You must call off the trip."

"No way."

"Mark beat me up last night."

"Because of Miou?"

"It was all my fault. I hadn't asked him and when he suddenly saw you standing there with her he felt he'd been side-stepped. I tried to explain, I apologized but that just made him even more angry."

"I'm awfully sorry about that, Tamara."

Tamara put the transport box next to Valerie's case.

"It would be better if you didn't fly anyway," Tamara said sheepishly. "I need you here. You are so right about Mark, and I don't think I can cope on my own."

Good old fate strikes back, thought Valerie. But wait a minute! Switch on your superbrain before you knuckle under!

"I know what we can do: you move into my place until Mark has calmed down, then Miou won't be alone either."

"But what about the dog? I can't bring him here and Mark can't take him out every day."

"You can take Alexander to the parents' place."

"They won't be able to cope with him."

"Then bring him here and leave Miou in Miriam's room. She will manage." Even more disturbing than the thought of Miou being locked up in one room for ten days was the thought that the boisterous boxer would take her house apart. But now Valerie did not care about that. All the signs pointed to Arizona and she was going to go!

"If I move out, Mark will blow his top. He will look everywhere for me and if he notices that I have only moved to your place because of the cat, he will kill her. He has already ..." Tamara stopped in mid-sentence and Valerie did not want to hear the end. Not now.

Tamara slumped into a chair, fell forwards onto the oak table top and wept uncontrollably.

"Move to the women's refuge and take Miou with you," Valerie said. "You'll be safe from Mark there."

Tamara's timing, Valerie thought, was perfect—as always. Apart from that she had apparently not closed the door of the transport box properly because Miou jumped out and ran off.

It was a virtual eternity before Tamara stopped crying. Valerie looked at her watch. In five minutes the taxi would be there and Miou had disappeared without trace. She tried to talk to Tamara even though she knew full well it was just a waste of time.

The taxi was at the door.

"Just one minute," Valerie said to the listless looking man who had got out to load her luggage. Part of her still hoped that Miou would reappear at the last moment and her sister would realize how serious things were.

At the end of the street a silver-grey Porsche Boxster loomed up. The passenger door was thrust open, Alexander jumped out baying wildly and backed Valerie up against the garden fence. Tamara seemed to have recognized the characteristic roar of the engine and appeared at the front door.

Mark, unshaven, smelling of sweat, loomed in front of Valerie. "I know you're behind all this," he said without further explanation.

"Behind what?"

He did not answer but stormed off to Tamara, grabbed her by the arm like a rabid dog and dragged her into his car. It was gruesome to watch her muscular, six-foot sister— who could have snapped her mini husband in half like a stalk of grass—being burnt down to a heap of ashes. The dog jumped into the back seat. Mark pushed Tamara onto the passenger seat and revved up the engine. Valerie stood there speechless. The final chord of Mark's spectacular performance consisted of him winding down the window and shouting across to Valerie:

"You'll pay for this!"

"For what?"

"I'll skin you alive and cut you into tiny blood-soaked scraps!"

The car sped away.

"Can we go then?" the taxi driver asked unmoved.

"My cat," Valerie said. "She's alone in the house."

"I have four cats alone in my house."

"But you're not going away for ten days." Valerie toyed with the idea of asking him whether he would take the cat to join his four, but the man stank of rotting cheese and she knew that Miou would loathe him.

The wind pressed the delicate stalks of spring grass flat against the ground in Valerie's front garden. Gitanes, my medicine horse!

"Just wait one minute," Valerie said and disappeared into the garden. 'Gitanes, you must rescue me from this god-awful mess. I want to go to America to discover the final secrets of humanity but can't even manage to find a place for my cat for a few days.'

She slumped down in her garden chair and closed her eyes. Mark danced before her inner eye and fired off his threats. Then Valerie saw a new-born child in a cradle. It was surrounded by people: men and women in clothes from a distant past. Valerie heard their voices: 'We are waiting for you.' The image had such intensity that all other feelings paled into insignificance.

"Thank you, Gitanes," Valerie said and stood up. "Miou!"

Her neighbour, an elderly woman who, because of her hunched back, barely reached up to Valerie's ribcage, was looking over the garden fence.

"She's with me," the lady said.

"I've got to go away for ten days," Valerie said. "I would happily pay you to look after my cat."

"That's not on," replied the neighbour. "The cat's all right but I'm not taking any money. Bring me back a postcard."

"I'll certainly do that," answered Valerie. "Give Miou the food that's on the kitchen unit twice a day. Here is the key."

Hallelujah, hallelujah, halleeeee-luuujaaah ...

12

22.00 hours, Mountain Standard Time, as they stepped out of Tucson Arizona airport into a warm wind, palm trees and cactuses. They set their watches back by eight hours and picked up the rented car. On the plane they had not sat next to one another because they had booked their flights separately, but now Tom was there. At his side Valerie felt like an orchid next to a hundred-year-old oak tree. Although she now knew him slightly better, she still found him awesome. Or was it not him but what he stood for, that mysterious something that she had come here to explore? Valerie so much wanted to be part of this sacred something that within its aura she hardly dared to breathe. You are summoning powers that you cannot control, Evi had warned her. Valerie resolved that, given the opportunity, she would apologize to Evi and admit that there were quite a few things that she really was unable to control.

It was late evening and they checked into the La Quinta airport hotel, each into their own room. The anonymous hotel room, the air conditioning, the spotless bathroom and the pile of sterile white towels seemed to Valerie like an island in the sea of mystery which was awaiting her. The next morning the sun rose with a heart-rending crimson that criss-crossed the sky in blood-red streaks. What the Americans fed their faces with could hardly be called breakfast, it was more an aberration of taste which claimed to be bagels and coffee, but which had surrendered all resistance to American body chemistry.

They had soon left behind the row of insipid, white-washed houses and the oversized neon billboards on the outskirts of Tucson, a city steam-rollered out of the wasteland. The SUV purred affectionately along the highway. Valerie hung her arm out of the open window and the radio music wafted out like a greeting to the incredible vastness around them.

Imperceptibly the landscape became more mountainous, more bizarre, treeless rock formations were silhouetted against the horizon, their forms like the history-book of an invisible narrator: the heads of noble Indian chiefs; people lying, standing, fleeing; animals with grotesquely contorted limbs, hands clasped in prayer, and rampant plants of stone. Valerie stared at the dashboard to check whether she could trust her perceptions, thinking the time shift had softened her brain and was tricking her with optical illusions. But when she looked out of the window again the heads of the Indian chiefs were still there in the rocks.

"All this seems very ... animated," she said to Tom.

"Has anyone welcomed you?" he replied as if this went without saying.

Valerie laughed. She held her arm out in the warm slipstream as if wanting to shake hands with one of the resident spirits.

Whoops! There really was somebody. IT was taking residence in Valerie's chest and grinning. "It feels good," she said trying to ignore the alarm bells of her intellect. But she was after all on holiday and *superbrain* was supposed to be taking a breather. She could let *superbrain* off the leash again when she got back.

"Who is it?" asked Tom.

"His colour is mint green—he is a water sprite," Valerie said as if it was the most normal thing on earth to talk about different-coloured spirits. "He said, if we need water, he'll take us to it."

"Very friendly of him," Tom answered. "Ask him what we can offer in return."

The spirit seemed to have been waiting for this question.

"He said the land had dried up and we should make rain."

Tom laughed heartily. "He seems to find us quite capable."

Valerie sighed. "That's a good beginning."

About an hour later they crossed a control point checking for illegal immigrants, the Mexican border was not far off. Tom and Valerie's German passports dispelled their doubts. Shortly afterwards they left the highway and turned onto a dusty track, the ground was as hard as concrete and ribbed, it felt as if they were driving over a washboard.

At what had once been the entrance to the plot of land lay a gate painted rust-red, it had been detached from its moorings or had simply fallen off. The other half of the gate was completely missing. Next to it Valerie noticed a sign lying with the inscription facing upwards in a heap of dried brushwood. It read: *Double T Bar Ranch.*

"What does the name mean?"

"They name their ranches after their brand."

"The Indians do that?"

"The Indians? No, the ranch owners." Tom's voice was as controlled as always.

The pick-up bounced over the rock-hard ground towards a clutter of dilapidated buildings. The area seemed deserted, which made it even more incredible that the extensive fields were dotted with horses and cattle. As they got closer Valerie noticed that the roof of one of the buildings had partially collapsed and the window panes had been smashed.

"What is this, a ghost ranch?" In a hollow lay three half-rusted pick-ups and a tractor, of which only a skeleton remained. One of the cars was so old that it could have been used in a gangster film from the forties. Around the ramshackle outhouses there were mountains of rubbish.

"What are we doing here?" Valerie asked. She felt a wave of despair, not because of the dilapidated buildings but because of the animals. She was afraid they were not getting enough to eat or drink. Why wasn't Tom answering her question?

He stopped in front of one of the buildings, turned off the engine and opened the car door. Valerie did not want to get out. Tom walked to the main building and disappeared through a door with a fly screen. He had not even turned round, let alone given her an explanation of what it was all about. It made her nervous that he was so abrupt. He was certainly cool, had this unassailable calm, yet he was anything but civilized. She decided to follow him. What else could she do?

A radio was blaring, in the half-light she saw a group of men sitting around a table staring darkly and a blonde woman in her forties, heavily made up and in a light blue jogging suit with a big glittery pink bunny on her chest. They greeted Tom as if he stopped by here every day. Nobody took any notice of Valerie. She had had a rather different image of the *tribe*, which was *waiting* for her here. But perhaps this was only the reception committee that was supposed to check on how genuine her intentions were. Valerie sat down on an available chair, away from the group. Tom opened a can of beer and offered it to her. This shook her to the core. Here am I thinking I am on my way to the holy Doors of Perception. Beer was the very last thing that could awaken Indian holiness within her. Something seemed to be going wrong here. Obviously she and Tom had misunderstood one another.

There he sat amongst his shifty companions and seemed to find everything completely normal.

"Is this the ranch we are going to spend a whole week on?" Valerie asked.

"I don't know."

At least he had answered her. Presumably the answer had also been honest.

The blonde woman started to talk about a trip to Dubai. Dubai of all places. Valerie tried to imagine what it would be like to fly to Dubai and in the lift of one of the most expensive hotels in the world meet a lady dressed like her. Obviously she had been there with a delegation of Indians who had Arab friends or whatever. It was to do with horse breeding, camels and falcons. Admittedly Tom's friends were the kind of exotic people you were not likely to come across in Schlattstall, but surely they were not people who could help her get over her grief about the death of her daughter. A feeling of helplessness overcame her as in the period just after Miriam's death, and she felt as if she was back at the starting point.

Somebody started frying hamburgers on a huge grill. At the back of the plain communal room they were in Valerie discovered a storeroom where provisions were kept. The blonde woman was tipping coleslaw from a bucket into a bowl. Valerie did not understand why these people had gathered together and why Tom had brought her here. She sat down in a corner and ate a hamburger with masses of barbecue sauce which soon lay heavy in her stomach.

It was getting dark. Tiredness overwhelmed her. Where

would they spend the night? Was the question important? Was anything important? Whether she was alive or dead? Totally unimportant. Since Miriam's death she would find the world an alien place for the rest of her life, no matter where or who she was with. This run-down ranch did not matter anymore.

"Hi!"

Valerie was jerked out of her drowsy thoughts.

"How are you," she replied in English. The blonde woman was standing in front of her, holding a beer can, and with enough alcohol on her breath to start a fire.

"We are going to sleep now," she said, "where do you want to sleep?"

"I'll sleep in this chair," Valerie replied. She didn't feel like following the blonde woman anywhere that a mattress might be waiting which was more worse-for-wear than the collapsed roof of the house.

"Okay," the blonde woman replied unmoved.

"Thank you anyway," said Valerie. She had probably just experienced the height of the helpfulness customary here. Valerie scanned the faces of the men who had stood up but Tom was not amongst them. She followed the men outside. Tom's pickup had vanished. How could she have possibly failed to notice that Tom had disappeared? She felt a surge of panic when she realized that she had been left all alone amongst these peculiar people. Evi had been right, there was no way that she was inwardly prepared for this adventure.

It was cold, even if not as cold as in Germany. She would spend the whole night freezing because the house was not heated. As quick as she could Valerie returned to the room to retain her body heat.

The only functioning light in the whole place flickered outside the window and prevented her from sleeping. Her tiredness had given way to a torturous wakefulness produced by her survival instinct. I can't sleep because a bear will possibly come striding in to raid the supplies, she thought. To keep out the cold Valerie draped a plastic sheet she had found in the supply room over the shattered window.

The digital clock on the fridge read 03.15. The approximately fifty-third wave of mammoth despair was rolling in. She would never reach forty, fifty or sixty with the thought that she had lost her daughter. The wound would never heal. That was certain, absolutely unshakable.

Valerie stepped through the door out into the night. In the fields she recognized the silhouettes of horses and, to her own amazement, the sight of them consoled her. She recognized a paint horse amongst them. *Oh my god ...* The horse turned to look at her, started to move and came walking towards her dragging his feet. A tough, powerful animal that did not waste its energy. It sniffed her and nudged her with its nose, lifted its head and demanded to have its chin scratched. Valerie ran her fingernails through its rough coat and followed its instructions. How strange that on an unknown ranch in the middle of nowhere she should be scratching the chin of an unknown horse and finding comfort in that. A horse's chin. Her eyes filled with tears. How insane that a horse could reduce her to tears. Valerie thought of how often Gitanes had made her cry. And how since then the itching in her eyes that she had suffered from for so long had almost disappeared. Something important that my eyes did not want to see ... and what did they see? A horse?

After he had had enough scratching, the paint turned his head in the direction of the hills around the ranch, most of them bare but some of them overgrown with waist-high underbrush. Valerie followed his gaze and saw a figure sitting at the top of a rise. Its silhouette melded with the lines of the landscape and yet stood out like an ornament. Judging by the delicate outline it seemed to be a woman sitting there cross-legged. An uncanny silence emanated from her which could be felt even at a distance. The horse flinched. It had noticed that Valerie had turned away. It raised its head and uttered a loud call, which echoed back from the slopes. Silence. Then a second call. And an answer. It came from the direction of the hill the woman was sitting on. A third call, an answer from several horses. The clip-clop of hooves, an uncanny sound, hard and dry, quiet at first then louder. In the dense cloud cover a gap opened and the full moon appeared behind it, its light surrounding the seated woman with a milky glow. Valerie's heart virtually stopped. Behind the woman a herd of horses in full gallop stampeded down the slope and then back up again. The horses' heads appeared behind her and seemed to be just about to trample over her. Valerie screamed. But the figure did not move.

The scream exploded from Valerie's throat, she ran off towards the figure to shake her but it was much too late. The first horse came looming up behind the woman, ran a circle round her and galloped down the slope to the paint horse. The other horses followed suit.

They gathered behind Valerie and a surge of energy flowed through her limbs like an electrifying current. She left the paint to his fellow horses and headed for the unknown woman, who emitted an inexplicable attraction. When she noticed that nothing had happened to the woman the relief Valerie felt was indescribable.

13

Her face was framed by a fur hood, beneath which two dark eyes glowed, set off from her white skin like black crystals. She was not an Indian and did not seem to belong to any other definable ethnic group. The proportions of her face reminded one of a Chinese jade doll but her lips and nose were European. Her age—hard to say.

"I am Valerie."

"My name is Salik," the stranger answered and smiled.

"Valerie Rosenstein."

"Salik Noor."

"What does your name mean?" Salik asked.

Valerie translated: "Roses and stone. What does your name mean?"

"Salik is Arabic and means freedom. My surname, Noor, is also Arabic and means light."

"Salik Noor."

Salik's hands were hidden in gloves but she offered to shake Valerie's hand anyway.

"Welcome."

"Why are you here?" Valerie asked.

"For the same reason as you."

"Were you also ... summoned?" Valerie said, uncertain whether she had gone too far.

"Yes," said Salik.

Valerie, who so far had been crouching, balanced on tiptoes, sat down next to Salik on the flat rock. Moonlight still illuminated the valley and Valerie felt as if she was wrapped in a coat of light. She liked Salik straight away. She thought she smelled of peaches although there were certainly no peaches in this area. The whole environment seemed to adopt a different character because of Salik's presence. As if the hills and mountains, the valley and the animals were only now revealing their true nature. Valerie wanted to say something, felt it on the tip of her tongue, but as soon as she tried to open her mouth, the words fled, she forgot what she wanted to say and the forgotten words made way for a deeper perception. Without wanting to Valerie sank into Salik's world which suffused everything with mild, delicate light.

Valerie did not know how long she had been sitting there but as it slowly grew lighter she noticed that the night was ending. A red wall of light rose beyond the mountain ridge.

"Can you see her?" Salik pointed to the peak of the mountain.

"Incredible," gasped Valerie. The figure of a sleeping woman was etched in the rock. It was the same one Valerie had unearthed while researching on the Internet.

Wright Peak.

"The Medicine Woman," Salik said.

"The Medicine Woman."

"This is her sacred land. The Apaches once lived here."

Salik turned to Valerie and looked at her with jet black eyes. Valerie scratched in the dust with her shoe, seized a stone lying there and absent-mindedly drew circles on the ground at her feet as if wanting to lure something from the depths of her memory with this movement.

"You are a member of the *tribe*," said Valerie.

"Me and seven other men and women," Salik answered.

"Tom included."

Salik nodded.

"Who are the others?"

"You met them yesterday afternoon."

"That—forgive me—that sorry lot?"

"Do not judge them. They are the descendants of a great people."

Valerie sighed. "Do you know where Tom has disappeared to?"

"He is still getting a few things we need for the ceremony."

"I've been feeling very lost this afternoon," Valerie said.

"You will understand."

"I've lost my daughter ... Miriam. She was killed by a horse." Valerie noticed a tightening in her chest and with the next breath a wave of burning pain flooded her body.

"I simply can't survive with all this pain."

"You'll be able find your strength again."

"I'm not a spiritual person like you."

"Everybody has a soul, don't you believe that?"

"Yes, of course," Valerie sighed again. She saw the paint horse heading for them.

Salik laughed. "His name is Seth."

"Isn't that the name of an Egyptian god?"

"A desert god who invokes storms and bad weather and is linked with the powers of chaos."

"Why have you ... I mean ... why has *the tribe,* called me? Or why do you call yourself a *tribe* at all—and why do I belong to it?"

"We need you."

"What for?"

"You don't know?"

"No."

Once again this peculiarly alien and yet familiar feeling which Valerie felt in Salik's presence surged within her.

The paint horse, Seth, trudged up the hill and stopped in front of them.

"There are some things that only horses have an answer for," Salik said and smiled cheerfully.

In sudden recognition Valerie pressed her fist to her mouth. "I haven't thought about it for at least twenty years. No idea why this suddenly occurs to me." She shook her head in disbelief. "When I was six, I fell in a river. We had climbed up a high tree with a branch that hung over the water ... I slipped. I couldn't swim and the river carried me off. There were whirlpools, I was sucked under. I was help-less, the current was too strong. I thought I was going to die. I haven't thought about that for a very long time, but now I realize that when this phone call from the stables came and the woman said, Miriam ... that was the same feel-ing, a feeling as if I was going to die."

"You survived."

Valerie hugged her knees, her whole body began to tremble violently. "That time, in the river. There was this light, it drew me magically towards it. I followed it and ..." Again Valerie pressed a hand to her mouth. "That is ... no! ..." Her words faltered. "I saw a man, an Indian with those feathers you see in book illustrations, large, colourful feath-ers all round his head. He was dressed in every colour of the rainbow. It was as if he could work magic. He had come to save my life." The memory had returned. To see that In-dian awakened a feeling of deep peace within her. "He showed me that I'm stronger than I think I am. Suddenly I had incredible strength. I came to the surface. And there was a branch and I clung to it. My friends came and pulled me out of the water. I lay there in my sopping-wet clothes and I felt totally happy. They couldn't understand it. They took me home and the Indian was with me the whole time. I thanked him for saving my life." Again Valerie pressed her fist to her mouth, her eyes flooding with tears, and it took some time before she could find her voice again. "I asked him if there was anything I could do to repay him."

Valerie opened her eyes. The horse was standing beside her, looking over her shoulder into the distance. She saw that Salik was listening to her attentively. "I think I'm beginning to understand something."

"We need you," said Salik. "You are the key, without you we cannot perform the ceremony."

"But how do you know about me? I live on the other side of the planet."

"Ask the horses."

Valerie looked up at the paint horse standing there dreamily, seemingly absorbed in pleasant visions. She thought of Gitanes and realized she was missing him. The red strip on the horizon spread over the whole sky, bathing the figure of the supine medicine woman in fire.

Valerie closed her eyes to hold on to the distant memory, even though she was no longer afraid of losing it.

"At that time, when I asked the Indian how I could thank him, I saw images of a landscape. A stony valley in a desert-like region very similar to the landscape here. The folds of the hills in that valley were however different, more finely chiseled as if created by a supreme artist. A solitary tree stood in the middle of the valley and in its shade lay a coiled snake. On the left, sunk in the rock face, was a cave and I saw the Indian heading towards it. He said: *Here dwells the light.* Then he disappeared into the cave." Valerie sighed deeply. "Isn't it incredible that I remember it all so exactly even though I was only six years old?"

"It is fascinating, our memory," Salik said and once again the mysterious smile played on her lips.

"The place where the light dwells, do you think it's here in this area?" Valerie asked, hardly really trusting her own words.

"Perhaps. Our brothers and sisters have been searching for it for a long time."

Valerie felt that she was moving in a world beyond anything that she had ever known or had believed. But here, with Salik, everything made sense. This was the only way it made sense. And what did it matter if—when seen in the light of day—all these things were crazy? She felt consolation and a feeling of having arrived, even if this home was the strangest place she could possibly imagine.

"To sum up," she continued soberly. "This Indian ..."

"Chief Black Falcon."

Valerie laughed. "Chief Black Falcon? Do you know him?"

"He was Tom's great grandfather ... and also my great grandfather ... and the other brothers' and sisters' great grandfather."

"But not my great grandfather ..."

"Do you know that?"

"I'm not a hundred per cent sure, of course ... I always thought my ancestors were ten generations of German cattle dealers and lawyers ..."

Again and again as her brain tried to process all this new information Valerie shuddered slightly.

She sighed. "So you've been waiting for me because you ... hoped I would help you find the place where the light dwells."

"We are helping one another. Isn't that so?"

Yes, thought Valerie. "I hope so."

"Good," said Salik. "Are you ready then?"

Valerie nodded.

14

Tom's pick up came clattering onto the yard and two of the men ran towards it.

Valerie greeted Tom, who nodded at her in a friendly way yet without giving her any explanation of where he had been all night. After all he did not owe her an explanation. Valerie and Salik followed him into the main house. The blonde woman and two Indian women were sitting there. Valerie had no idea why these people—who the day before had ignored her—suddenly stood up and greeted her. Had Salik given them some sign? Or had they noticed in some telepathic way that she had become more open? By this time Valerie had come to consider almost anything possible. She was bleary from lack of sleep and her mind was only working in emergency mode. In its place a vague madness had set in, which flared up of its own accord. Premonitions, telepathy, chains of meaning which stretched back thirty years—anything was possible. Names, places, occurrences, everything apparently contained a double meaning. A horse named Seth functioned as a messenger of chaos, and a woman called Salik Noor, representing the freedom of light, turned out to be—together with the rest of the bunch—a great-great-grand-child of the deceased Indian chief Black Falcon, who had saved her—Valerie's—life when she was a six-year-old child in Habichtswald near Kassel.

"My name is Donna. Do you want a coffee?" The blonde woman thrust a porcelain cup with a broken handle into her hand. It made Valerie nervous that there appeared to be nothing in this place that was intact.

"Hi, I'm Karma," said one of the Indian women. "Don't be surprised by my name, my father was a hippie." Karma must have been about thirty. Her virtually lidless eyes were set like dark buttons in her reddish brown skin and had that fixed, distant stare of an owl. Karma smiled briefly and Valerie noticed that one of her front teeth was broken off. Apart from that she came across as friendly, gentle and compliant, and she awakened Valerie's protective instincts. The other Indian woman came up to Valerie with strange formality.

"I am Lauren Lott." With eyes lowered she offered Valerie her hand. Lauren was perhaps forty, though it was hard to tell given that she was overweight. Her black hair hung in strands over her face, there was a scar across her left cheek. She was wearing jeans, cowboy boots and a pink, quilted anorak. She seemed shy and somewhat stiff but on closer appraisal Valerie noticed an underlying nervousness. Puzzled Valerie released Lauren's hand.

In the meantime the other two Indian men had come into the room. The smaller and elder of the two raised his hand. "Chuck," he said and grinned. "I'm the wrangler." He expressed this with a half proud, half ironic undertone. 'Wrangler'—this had penetrated even as far as Valerie— was not the inventor of jeans but the term used for the man responsible for the horses.

"This is my son Alfred," Chuck went on. "You have Alfreds in Germany, don't you?" He laughed. His laughter sounded fresh and healthy, oxygen-enriched by wind and weather. Confronted with this down-to-earth and practical Chuck and what appeared to be his equally matter-of-fact son, Alfred, Valerie immediately felt slightly better. Both men had pure Indian features: dark skin, lidless black eyes, broad noses, full reddish brown lips and high cheek bones—and they epitomized work.

"Have you already met Derek?" asked Chuck and glanced to the end of the table where a broad-shouldered man was sitting like an immovable block of wood and devouring fried eggs as if they were the last things he was ever going to eat before being executed.

"Hi, Derek," said Valerie.

Derek did not react.

"He is not exactly talkative," said Chuck.

"Do you all live here on the ranch?"

"Alfred and I look after things. The ranch belongs to an estate agent who has been trying to sell it for years. But hereabouts any number of ranches are up for sale."

"So you've all come together just for this *purpose*?" Valerie was trying to get the lay of the land.

"Well, yeah." Chuck seemed lost for words.

"Ah, doesn't really matter," said Valerie.

"Do you want some breakfast?" asked Chuck, apparently the personification of courtesy.

"I'd prefer a bed. I'm so tired I can hardly stand upright. I hardly slept a wink last night."

Salik said, "I don't believe that's possible."

Valerie had suspected as much. It would have surprised her if she had found compassion, consolation or any other form of human kindness in this place.

"What's the plan," she asked soberly.

"There's a full moon. So it has to happen tonight."

"What?" Valerie braced herself for anything.

Nobody answered. Any other reaction would have surprised Valerie. It would have been easier to get Chief Black Falcon to answer from the Beyond. And yet behind this very silence there seemed to lurk a secretive conspiracy amongst those present.

"That means ... ," Valerie expressed Salik's thoughts aloud.

Salik finished the sentence: "We ride off as soon as possible."

"I have only ever ridden once in my whole life," Valerie said and a wave of panic closed over her, which, however, ebbed away on the beach of her leaden tiredness.

"If you can sit on a chair, you can sit on a horse," said Chuck, and the fried-egg-man, Derek, took pleasure in laughing quietly to himself.

"Thank you," Valerie answered.

"You'll be ok," said Salik with the same conviction as the day before when she had simply sat there as the herd of horses had galloped past her.

"It's all predetermined anyway," said Valerie and could not suppress insane laughter. This did not seem to bother the others at all. What a bunch of ... !

"The gods are bastards," said Donna.

Lauren countered: "The spirits are hungry."

Chuck said to Valerie, "in these circumstances I would recommend a hearty breakfast." And with unexpected helpfulness Lauren peeled a paper plate from a pile and loaded it with eggs, untoasted toast, slices of pickled cucumber and a huge dollop of ketchup which buried everything like a burst bag of donated blood.

Tom heaved a western saddle onto Seth's powerful back and threaded the strap. He said to Valerie, "You're putting up a good show." As he tightened the belt Seth gave a deep sigh. "I admire your courage."

"To label it 'courage' is an exaggeration. 'Tiredness' I call it. Jetlag, a sleepless night and a total lack of hope about whether I'll come through this alive, but, anyway, that's not important."

Valerie grinned crookedly.

"That's the very courage I mean."

Their eyes met. Without words.

Seth, the plucky paint, snorted contentedly. Valerie laid her hand on his neck. "I like him," she said. "He could be Gitanes' little brother."

Tom grinned. "He is a tough cookie, you'll soon see."

"How long will we take?"

"I don't know," Tom answered and Valerie believed he really meant it. Into her saddle bags he packed bottles of water, a bag of bread for toasting and a supply of sliced cheese and ham.

"You never know on this kind of trip."

The others had also saddled their horses, Alfred, the wrangler's son, was on a wiry black horse which only seemed to know two forms of movement: full gallop and standing still. Salik was riding a glistening red mare with slim legs and such a beautiful head that it should have been cast in bronze. They both fitted together perfectly. Chuck was on a matted, stubborn-looking horse but it looked like a real survivor. The other horses seemed relatively calm.

Without anyone giving any kind of signal the troop set off. Valerie noticed that up till now nobody had taken on the role of leader. How much did the others know, or to put it differently: what ideas did the others have of where their journey was to lead them? Valerie had the feeling that none of them knew much more than she did herself. How could they be so confident that all this made sense and that they would achieve their goal?

On his nervous, black horse Alfred tirelessly galloped up and down the line of trotting horses as if they had to check that everything was in order. It impressed Valerie that the other horses were not affected by this, they were apparently very self-assured.

Their aim—at least that is what Valerie assumed—was the valley that Chief Black Falcon had revealed to her in that vision thirty years before. But perhaps she had got it all wrong. In any case the group seemed to feel no need to discuss anything; as Valerie had read in various books, given that they were all Indians and related to one another, they were perhaps also genetically wired to communicate telepathically. But how did they know which direction to take to reach the valley? East, west, north, south. Was it blasphemous that she at least—as a non-Indian and a reasoning European—wanted to have a goal in mind? The lethargic pace of the paint horse made sure that this questioning and other power struggles of her reason got lost in the white fleecy clouds across the light-blue sky.

They were following a track which seemed to be frequently used for rides or walks because it was well and truly trampled flat. At half past nine the track became steeper and at eleven they reached a rise which revealed a view in all directions. Beautiful, bizarre, the rock silhouette, enormous cactuses, a stream flowing down through the valley, uninhabited, primeval.

Chuck, who had ridden on ahead, drew up his horse and the group formed a circle. All eyes turned to Valerie.

"Which way?" asked Chuck in that sober fashion of his which left no room for ambiguity.

"You're asking me?" said Valerie disconcerted. She leant back, her hand resting on Seth's rear and turned first to the left, then to the right. It came to her that she was the only one amongst those present who did not know the area. Why were they asking her of all people? In none of the four directions was there anything she could discover that might have helped her make a decision. *Seek not without but within,* where had she read that? But there was no answer—neither within nor without.

"I have no idea," she said finally. "I'm sorry."

Chuck sighed. "Never mind," he said. "No reason to despair."

"Who cares?" said Derek and rode off to the east. The others followed him. Valerie could not imagine that Derek had the foggiest idea what he was doing. But then who *does* care?

Seth, the thunder god, started to move as well.

15

The sun was reaching its full height and they had spent the whole morning riding more or less aimlessly round the area. It was Valerie's first major ride and apart from the fact that nobody knew where they were going it was even fun. Up one hill, a magnificent view, crossing a valley like Winnetou und Old Shatterhand, an eagle circling and sending signals, holding your silver rifle at the ready, appealing to Manitu for the battle to end in your favour. Plunging into a gnarled oak wood with the branches whipping in your face, an Indian feels no pain, coming back into the sun lacerated, having the sun burn on your back, and wishing never to return to the world of atom bombs, cosmetic surgery and hedgefonds.

How had the sun returned to the horizon so quickly, was it already worn out? Hey, how are we going to get back without the main spotlight? Valerie was too tired to think about the question of where she was going to spend the night and how far the return journey was going to be and she sank a bit lower in her saddle, which seemed to offer almost endless new depths.

Perhaps I will be rescued from the wilderness by a helicopter and end up in the German headlines: *German woman, kidnapped by a group of escaped psychopaths in America, the land of endless possibilities.* Sliced open and disembowelled in a satanic ritual. The whole population of

Schlattstall would think: how stupid can you be? Every moron knows that you don't get involved in that sort of thing.

The valley really looked exactly as it had in her vision thirty years before. The human memory was phenomenal, there's no doubt about that. Every fibre of her body was vibrating. She squinted but the impression remained. She knew this place. And knew it well. She was gripped by crazy internal excitement. The rock faces, the isolated tree—and the cave. It was all exactly as it had been in her vision.

Salik came riding up on her elegant sorrel mare and stopped beside Valerie. Seth was quite a bit smaller than the mare and Valerie had to look up at Salik. No words were necessary, just one look and a hardly perceptible nod. The look Salik answered with expressed something like: you really can!

"Here it is!" shouted Salik to the others.

Valerie was proud of their wordless exchange, of the fact that this valley really existed and she felt a surge of Indian blood flowing through her veins, whether it was genetically possible or not.

"What do we do now?" asked Valerie.

"We ride down."

The trail into the valley was stony and the horses kept slipping over the scree.

"An apple tree," yelled Derek. "Have you ever seen anything like it? In the desert?" The others were astonished, too.

They dismounted. Chuck and Alfred took over the horses. They unpacked their bread, cheese and sausage and ate. They talked about horses, about the fact that the estate agent's new wife was always buying more horses. "No idea what she's planning to do with them," said Lauren. "Some women have a cupboard full of shoes. She has a ranch full of horses."

"I like the horses she brings."

"Yes, she has taste. I only hope she has enough money to feed them."

Valerie found out that the grass on the wide-spread fields did not suffice, that they had to import hay from California which was barely affordable.

Lauren worked in a souvenir shop in a tourist town called Patagonia. That is where she always got the latest gossip about the area. Apart from that she was often a guest at the local psychiatric clinic. "The only place you meet normal people," she said. "I am obsessed with my passion," she continued.

"What passion?" Valerie wanted to know.

"Painting." As if to prove this she drew a figure in the sand with her finger. "Horses." The drawing showed a horse with a completely individual expression.

"It is Easy," shouted Karma. Valerie glanced across to the brown horse that Lauren had ridden and really did recognize him from the drawing. "That's why I like hanging around the ranch, even if it is the most desolate place in the whole region. Lots of horses." She erased the image with her fingers.

The atmosphere was more relaxed than ever. "Why are you in this group, Lauren?"

Lauren flinched. Apparently Valerie's question had touched a raw nerve. Her eyes narrowed, then her expression became sad. "Three hundred years ago we lived in this country, free and independent. We were at one with the spirits. Nowadays lots of people talk about the spirits, everybody has visions and whatever. But how can a spirit come here with it looking so ugly? Take a look at my body. Do you think any spirit would want to visit this body? No. I eat and eat, and drink and drink because I have a hunger that no food can satisfy. The food that I eat is not food, and the water I drink is poisoned. It is making me ill. Nobody can live here and remain healthy and receive spirits. Do you understand that, German lady? I hope none of you are so ill."

"I don't know ... are you here today to ... meet a spirit?"

Lauren threw back her head proudly. "I'm here to bring my soul back home."

"My parents smoked a lot of marihuana," said Karma abruptly. "Their life was not good, they had no home, always moved on, had no work and no money. But they created something beautiful in my soul ... my father always said, you have to find your tribe. We found one another via the Internet. We are all descendants of Chief Black Falcon. This is my tribe: Lauren, Salik, Tom, Chuck, Alfred, Derek, Donna ... and you, German lady."

"Why me?" Valerie asked.

Karma smiled: "Ask the horses."

"My name is Valerie."

"Valerie." Karma smiled modestly. "The spirits have brought us together to complete the sacred circle. From this circle a new energy will arise which will radiate out into the world." The delicate-looking woman suddenly seemed fiery and strong. "Why are you here, Valerie?"

"I lost my daughter, Miriam. She died six months ago." Valerie paused and wrung her hands. "I wasn't able to say farewell to her."

Karma nodded, as if she knew what Valerie was talking about.

All this time Derek had been sitting there, looking inward. "I hate the Germans. Nazis," he said. "They gassed everybody who didn't have white skin and blue eyes."

"Have you ever been to Germany?" asked Valerie.

"No."

Valerie felt uncomfortable.

"Do you hate the Indians, too, Derek?" Tom asked

smugly.

"Oh yes!"

"And the Chinese?"

"Bloody bastards!"

"And the Americans?"

"They are a great nation."

"Are you American?"

"I certainly am."

"He is pissed off because I insulted the air and the water on American soil," said Lauren. "I hate white Americans."

Valerie had expected that now, they had found the valley, and—after all that was virtually a miracle—a kind of holy mood would set in. But here they were discussing things on the level of a soap opera. It gradually went dark, the last rays of sunlight disappeared beyond the horizon and an unpleasant coolness spread.

The cave, thought Valerie, before I freeze to death tonight, I have to at least see the cave.

When she tried to stand up, her legs drew her down again like sacks of sand. To walk up there, to climb the slope? Impossible.

But that was what everything depended on. The question was: was it all imagination or would they actually find the *light* here that Chief Black Falcon had talked about.

Everything fitted, the slight projection, about four metres wide and two metres deep, the cave at head height as the Indian had shown it to her. This is where Black Falcon had stood. Yet the opening in the rock, through which he had disappeared, did not exist. The back wall of the cave consisted of mute stone, viewed from here at least.

Irresistibly Valerie was drawn towards it, she wiped the crumbs of her cheese sandwich from the corners of her mouth and forced herself upright with the last ounce of her strength.

"I'll be back," she said. But after the first few steps an indescribable tiredness overwhelmed her and she sank to the hard stone floor. I will never get there, she thought. Never … As the last sunlight faded, all colour was drained from the environment and her eyes closed.

16

This is what it must be like to die: a vast, clear, star-spangled sky, infinite space that swallowed her up. Her body consisted of countless, tiny parts which dissolved in the immensity. She consisted of dust. Just dust.

She recognized Tom, Donna, Salik, Derek, Chuck, Alfred, Lauren and Karma. They formed a circle around her, their faces lit by the moonlight. Lauren had a feather in her hair, black and white. Salik was encapsulated in light, Tom wore the stone countenance of an Indian. When we die, we can see the essence of all beings, she thought. The group was humming a soft melody. Derek was shaking a rattle, Donna was clapping her hands and rocking her heavy body back and forth to the rhythm.

Valerie saw that she was lying on a blanket, two paces away from the apple tree. The circle they had formed was imbued with a devoted sadness which tore larger and larger fragments of despair from Valerie's soul and hurled them out into the universe. That was what it felt like to die. A whirling kaleidoscope of images moved past, as if somebody had stirred the archives of her memory. Had they somehow drugged her? Or was it sheer exhaustion? It was as if her soul was throwing off old clothes at the speed of light and putting on new ones, only to throw these off, too. Merely in order to penetrate to this naked core where everything came to a standstill. Where death was complete.

But for now there seemed to be no end in sight and she felt completely at the mercy of this process.

While she had this feeling of dying inwardly, she felt for brief moments an urge to return to life which was surprisingly strong. Yet not strong enough to put up any resistance to the power of death. She tried to resist with tooth and claw but it was futile and she collapsed like a new-born baby and wept with tiredness, with exhaustion.

"What have you done to me?" she shouted at the others but received no answer. The chanting had changed colour and the rhythm of the rattle was gathering speed. A drum joined in, stamping, shouts, an ecstatic wave was building up and carrying her along.

I'm not alone—this insight came abruptly to her—they're talking to me through their drumming, their chanting. They know me, they know who I am at the very depths of my soul.

They know now that I am responsible for Miriam's death. I wasn't looking after her properly. I allowed her to ride that murderous horse, Korbas, who trampled her to death. I allowed her to die that horribly painful death, crushed by the hooves of a savage animal. I gave birth to her only to allow her to die in agony when her life had barely begun. I trod her innocence under foot, I did not protect her. I do not deserve to go on living. How can I live when she had to die?

The drumming and the voices had become very loud now, they came thick and fast like the screams of untamed animals. I've no right to live. I have simply no right to live. It is true. It is the law. I have killed so I must die. It is the law of my very soul.

After Valerie had realized this, she became calmer. A kind of peace settled in, the chanting ebbed away until it became almost completely silent. Time flowed on like calm waters. Valerie's breathing slowed, became calm. She drew in the smell of the damp night air. The fine chirping of the crickets drowned the human humming. It did her good to perceive the real world after life had abandoned her, a strange contradiction which at the same time made complete sense. A feeling of gratitude swept through her for having been allowed to experience this. She felt as if she had been invited by a generous, gentle mother who cared for her. Can she save me? she asked herself. Do more such beings dwell in these rocks? Had the spirits awoken? She heard Lauren murmuring words in a foreign language and felt deeply consoled by the thought that Lauren knew these spirits and was talking to them.

As yet this nameless thing had no face. Now she felt quite clearly that there was something present. She could not see it but she became quite animated.

"Miriam!"

Valerie sat bolt upright and glanced in the direction of the apple tree. There stood the child. She could vaguely perceive her outline, it was vibrating, it was energy rather than tangible form. A concentration of bluish-white light. And next to her the horse, Seth, the paint. When Valerie looked more closely, she saw that Miriam was holding a snake in her hand. The snake that Valerie had seen in her vision thirty years before, when she had first been in this valley.

Only now did the meaning of the snake become clear. The snake of transformation. Why was the child holding it in her hands?

As if Miriam had understood the question, she raised the snake held it up high. Here—Valerie thought she heard the child say—I give you life.

How can you give me life when you have lost it? Valerie seemed unable to find a solution to this contradiction but it did not bother Miriam.

I give you life, she repeated.

Me? I cannot accept this gift. I do not deserve it. I deserve death.

There is no death, answered the child. How else could I be here?

The answer confused Valerie. Again she had the feeling that her ego was disintegrating as if everything was being sucked down into the great all-consuming maelstrom. The child was still standing there in her total innocence. She was not angry, demanded no revenge. Wanted no sacrifice.

Valerie's heart was suffused with love for the girl. She felt as connected to Miriam as she always had, as if nothing had happened, as if she were still alive. And the girl returned her love. Yes, the love between them was complete, as it had always been, love between a mother and her child. Great and pure, Valerie was overwhelmed by it.

You still don't understand it, she thought she heard Miriam say. This did not sound reproachful or impatient, it sounded as if she would go on standing there until Valerie understood, as if she had all the time in the world.

What am I to understand?

Then Valerie gave up all resistance, gave up all questioning and allowed herself to surrender to this love. How all-encompassing it was. It did not just include Valerie and Miriam, but all human beings, animals, plants, and even stones, the air, the water—everything that existed. Valerie swam in this love as if in a vast, warm sea, she forgot all her pain, all her mourning, there was just this single tremendous feeling of happiness, this endless, consoling, blissful love which she wished would never ever fade.

17

Miriam and Valerie had exchanged places. Valerie was now standing beside the apple tree, Seth, the paint, beside her. And in the middle of the circle stood Miriam. As if she, Valerie, had merely been the gate through which the child had entered.

Now she realized that the spirit of the child was much larger than she had suspected. The child had come to the people who had gathered here. Valerie was astonished by the huge web that was stretched above them all. She now saw the horses approaching, attracted by the Light Being. Could they see her, too? They stopped close to the circle, snorted, their heads raised with curiosity, their ears in motion.

The child offered the snake to Tom and Valerie realized that he was the leader. He had brought the group together, he was the connecting link. Could anyone else see all this? Or she alone? But that was not important now. Karma raised her hand to catch the child's attention but it did not react. Again and again the delicate, fragile Indian woman lifted her hand as if she was afraid of remaining invisible. Why did the messenger show no mercy?

One of the horses, the stubborn gelding that Chuck had ridden, swayed over to Karma and pushed her in the back with his head so that she stumbled forwards. She turned round and looked at the horse in astonishment. It looked as if the horse had come to make clear to her that she was visible—to him. Now Karma was calm. It seemed as if the horses were working together with the messenger. Would all the people present receive a message, Valerie wondered. The way she had been given love?

Valerie looked around the valley. She had never taken part in such a ceremony before and she had expected something completely different. She had also believed that she would be completely absorbed as in a dream. But her sense of reality was still working. She could recognize everything clearly: the tree, the valley, the horses, the people. Except that the valley had gained something like a second reality. Before it had just been stone, and now it possessed something like a presence. It appeared as a bowl, a vessel or a divine womb. Valerie felt as if she could feel the millennia-old spirits of the people who had lived here and performed ceremonies. Had Chief Black Falcon lived here? Definitely. He had come straight from this valley to her river in Habichtswald near Kassel and had rescued her and in doing so had brought this place close to her and in a mysterious way had seen to it that she was now here in flesh and blood experiencing this ceremony.

Valerie directed her attention back to the group. Miriam, not the bodily Miriam, but the Light Being, was still in the same position, spiritually visible and yet invisible, her gaze directed to the south. The horses stood in a cluster next to the human circle, their heads bowed as if they, too, were captivated by the holy atmosphere. With their watchfulness the horses appeared to form something like a vessel similar to the valley, a power which enveloped and protected the people.

Lauren sighed loudly and shook herself, as if she wanted to throw off something unpleasant. Then she dropped to her knees, her hands covering her face and shook herself again and again.

Valerie became aware that she was still standing outside the group and she felt that it was time to become part of the circle again and to be there to support Lauren. Chuck and Alfred broke the circle and received Valerie like a fish joining its shoal. She immediately felt the strong bond within the group. That afternoon Lauren had spoken of the poison that was in the air, in the food and in people's souls. It looked as if her movements were shaking off the poison or dispelling it. Valerie, too, became aware of the poison in her body and, affected by Lauren, her body likewise began to shake as if it were a dusty carpet. Derek's arms began to flail wildly about and his body convulsed out of control. Valerie became slightly anxious that he would lose his mind. Then she told herself that the child was here after all, protecting her. Miriam seemed to know what was happening. The others, too, were shaking themselves and stamping and the energy in the circle grew considerably. Valerie let herself be carried along. As a group they were able to create more energy than an individual could have and the energy worked like a tremendous cleansing power, rather like a waterfall which took with it poison and dirt and painful feelings. Valerie looked at the horses to see whether they were disturbed by the intense movements but they were still standing there motionless. On the contrary, they seemed to be more concentrated and attentive, as if they, too, felt a waterfall pouring over them and experienced purification. Had the animals the same ability to perceive these things as humans do? Yes, Valerie thought. This seemed to be the climax. There were no words to express everything that was going on in the souls of those involved. Everything that had been confused before, seemed to be coming back into balance, everything seemed to be transformed into a condition of perfect harmony. Valerie felt that the individuals had been absorbed into the group, they were part of it and nonetheless they were still present as individuals. Together with the horses the humans formed a herd. This was clearly the climax of the ceremony, the purpose for which they had gathered together.

Derek moved out of the group and went up to the horse that he had ridden, a dark brown, sturdy horse with the saddest of eyes. It nosed at his hand, then turned round and ran off. Valerie felt the deep sadness that descended on Derek and wondered why the horse had run away from him. He stumbled off after the horse. Eventually he stopped and dropped to his knees as if he had collapsed. He seemed to have arrived at the lowest point of his sadness. The horse stopped and turned around with curiosity. Then it came trotting up to him and touched Derek's head with its muzzle. It was very moving to watch. Finally Derek got up, put his hand on the horse's withers and with the horse accompanying him, he came back into the circle.

Next Karma, the hippie girl, got up and went to the horses. As she approached them, they started to move but instead of running off they came up to Karma. Karma stretched out her arms to keep them away from her but they nuzzled and crowded her. Then Valerie saw the child joining Karma, it looked as if she had kindled a light in Karma and suddenly the young woman was surrounded by a power that apparently was also perceived by the horses because they left Karma alone. She now looked strong and self-contained, she jumped in the air a couple of times from pure joy, then she returned to the group. Valerie was astonished by the transformation that had come over both, Karma and Derek. Their facial expressions had changed. They seemed calm and contented and a hidden beauty became apparent.

Donna, Chuck and Alfred followed. They all experienced

a transformation which refreshed and filled them with joy. That only left Salik and Tom.

Salik moved amongst the horses like an ethereal figure of light. Valerie had never seen anything like it. The horses gathered around Salik as if around something infinitely sweet and exhilarating. The expression on their faces became dreamy, almost holy and even Salik's appearance became even more ethereal, more delicate and fine. She seemed to be thoroughly enjoying the whole experience.

Gradually the power of the energy, the disruption, the cramp, the upheavals and disturbances in the group diminished, because the individuals in the group gradually found more and more harmony. The ceremony seemed to be coming to an end, to be approaching resolution.

Valerie saw Tom move out of the circle. He went up to the horse he had been riding, a large brown gelding. There was something tortured in Tom's expression. He grabbed a handful of the horse's mane and swung up onto its back. He urged the horse to the human circle and took up his original position there, except this time up on the horse.

Valerie did not understand what this action meant. Until she saw the snake in Miriam's hand being transformed into a kind of sword and then transferred from the child's hand to Tom's. There he sat, up on the horse, with the sword in his hand like St. Michael, thought Valerie and was reminded of the picture hanging in her grandmother's bedroom. The moment he held the sword in his hand his body shone with light.

This seemed to be the sign for breaking up, because the child left the circle and accompanied by Tom, the knight, it moved towards the cave into which Valerie had seen Chief Black Falcon disappear. And just as Black Falcon had disappeared the previous time the child now disappeared through the back wall of the cave. So that was the secret.

The rock wall was the gateway to another reality, but only particular beings at a particular moment had access to it. Valerie felt great contentment.

Tom returned, dismounted from his horse and the group again began to clap and sing, this time in a mild, sweet tone until their voices gradually ebbed away. Tom ended the ritual with words in his Indian language. He bowed in all four directions and at each one scattered a handful of desert dust. All bowed to the centre of the circle, then the circle broke up.

Salik handed Valerie a blanket who wrapped herself up in it, lay down on the bare ground and immediately fell asleep.

18

"What time is it?" Valerie asked confusedly and pulled back the sleeve of her jacket to look at her watch. Eight.

She saw that the others had made a fire and were heating a billy can.

"Coffee! ... Here in the wilderness!"

"Absolutely," Lauren replied.

"Good grief, have I slept till now?" Valerie asked.

"I hope you've recovered."

Valerie folded up the blanket, dusted off her jeans and headed towards the fire. Despite having spent the night on the bare ground, she felt astonishingly refreshed.

"Morning, Tom."

"How are you?" he replied and handed her a tin cup. "Careful, it's hot."

Valerie pulled the sleeve of her pullover down over her fingers and reached for the cup.

"That does you good."

She looked around. The horses were searching on the rocky ground for individual stalks of grass. Chuck and Alfred were standing with them, making sure they did not run off.

Karma, Donna, Salik and Derek seemed just as sober as Chuck and Alfred, Tom and Lauren. It seemed to be a day like any other and from outside they probably just looked like a group of trekkers taking a rest.

The sun was shining pleasantly warm, there was a slight breeze and in Valerie's heart there slumbered a secret like a magic bud. She smiled silently to herself.

In the late morning they rode back to the *Double T Bar Ranch* without talking much; from time to time they just swapped comments about the direction, which, however, largely depended on the position of the sun. The memory of the night's events swept over Valerie like waves in a liquid which shimmered in all the colours of the rainbow and reached to the very roots of her hair. Seth snorted with unrestrained well-being.

For the rest of the day they hung around the ranch tired and listless. Derek fried hamburgers. Lauren opened a folding chair at the edge of the enclosure and did some drawing. Valerie wandered around the ranch, joined the horses and soaked up their uniqueness. She was astonished to see that they welcomed her visit, could not get enough of it. Then she lay down on a weathered bench, folded her anorak under her head and meditated with the stone medicine woman in the mountains. She christened her *Pachamama* an Indian goddess she had once heard of, and she liked the sounds: *pacha* and *mama*, a mother guarding her *pachas*. Pachamama poured wisdom over Valerie as if it cost nothing, Valerie felt as if she was part of an effervescent mountain spring whose sounds contained all the secrets of existence. It still felt like a vast internal purification and Valerie felt nothing but sheer astonishment.

"Everything OK?" asked Salik who had now joined her. Valerie nodded. "It'll take some time to digest everything. It seems to me like a dream but I know it wasn't one."

"If you ever have doubts, send me an e-mail. You'll find me on the Internet under my name."

"I get the feeling that there's not much left of what I once was—or my world once was."

"You have seen things as they are."

"No one will believe me."

"Does that matter?"

"No. It is enough that I've experienced it. I'm very happy and grateful to you all."

Valerie had four more days before her flight back was due. It was good to be so far away from home, to have no obligations, to hover between worlds. Although the range of food on the ranch was not exactly mouth-watering and the sofa next to the fridge with its constant death rattle was the only place to sleep, she enjoyed being with them all for a bit longer: Salik, Karma, Lauren, Chuck, Alfred, Donna, Derek and Tom, she enjoyed playing cards, feeding the horses and carrying on ambiguous discussions with Salik about the world beyond the curtain. On the third evening Valerie invited the whole group to the nearest steak house and presented each of them a key ring in the shape of a horse which she had bought in Lauren's souvenir shop.

"You will always be my brothers and sisters," Valerie said with a mouthful of chips, and they toasted one another with their glasses of beer while Johnny Cash sang *Ring of Fire* in the background.

"Have you got a horse?" Chuck asked Valerie the following morning while she was helping him distribute hay.

"No, and I don't intend to get one either."

"Everybody should have a horse," Chuck said. "Then the world would be a better place."

Valerie looked at him, his weathered skin, the gleam in his eyes, his stability, and she thought he was right.

On the last evening Salik invited Valerie to come up the hill where they had first met. They watched the sun go down.

"You are my *soul sister*," Salik said, a word which is hard to translate but is a beautiful word.

"This was just the beginning," said Valerie. "It seems to me as if my non-existent future has become a panorama with the sun rising."

"I admire you," Salik said.

"Me? No, I admire *you*. You *know* the light, I've hardly had more than a tiny glimpse."

"Do you think it's important to measure oneself and to compare?"

Valerie cocked her head. "No." She grinned. "But I'm happy to have met you. I don't know anybody like you." Valerie smiled and they embraced like sisters.

The next morning Tom took Valerie to the airport at Tucson. He would fly back a couple of days later, he still had something to sort out, he said. Precisely what, he did not disclose.

"Many thanks for taking me with you, Tom. This journey has changed my life. I feel you've all given me so much, thank you."

She embraced Tom. It was the first time she'd been so close to him physically but it felt right, it was not artificial or forced. I love you, she could have said in a totally innocent sense but perhaps it would have come across wrongly. I think he realizes that anyway, Valerie thought and blinked at him.

"We'll meet again," Tom said and Valerie waved until she had disappeared through the gate.

19

Spring had finally triumphed, everywhere there was green emerging, everything was burgeoning, and on the meadows grass was beginning to grow and individual trees were reaching out with an explosion of blossoms from the sea of green tones. Valerie turned into the farm yard and parked her car next to a claret red VW estate waggon with the name *Alexander Hausch* and the Internet address of his insurance office plastered on the back.

She looked around, marched between the stable and the dung heap in the direction of the riding paddock. A man was lunging a large, dark-brown horse which, as she approached, she immediately recognized.

"Hello."

This long-legged man's movements had a youthful charm and his face had an expression which could not fail to have a friendly effect on anybody, even though there was a certain melancholy beneath the surface. He walked up to the horse, rolled up the lunging rope and removed it from the halter. Korbas stood there motionless, looking in Valerie's direction.

When Alexander Hausch came closer, this melancholic trait was intensified, it was not, however, unpleasant, it was engaging, just like his friendliness, so that you enjoyed being in his presence, even though he did not appear to be aware of this.

"Mrs Rosenstein." He shook her hand with surprising strength.

"Hello, Mr Hausch. Thank you for finding the time."

"There is no need to thank me."

"I should have come before ..."

"I understand."

Valerie sensed that he was nervous. Before her Arizona trip, she would have found it inconceivable to meet the horse owner, to confront in any way the reality around Miriam's death, to face what exactly had happened. The very thought of it had triggered a panic attack. For this reason she had felt cowardly, had felt that she was leaving Miriam in the lurch once again, but now she was ready to open her eyes and look.

"It's not altogether easy ...," Alexander Hausch said.

Valerie cleared her throat. She had expected him to show some reserve, after all it had been his horse that had Miriam on its conscience, but his pain seemed to be similarly great and he made no attempt to hide it.

He leant back against the bar surrounding the paddock and, like Valerie, looked towards the horse which was still standing in the centre as if deserted, and seemed unclear about what it wanted, or was expected to do.

A silence spread which made formal greetings and introductions superfluous.

"He's not a killer," Alexander Hausch said.

The word twisted like a knife in Valerie's intestines.

"My god, I rescued him from a stable where he had been standing for months in almost total darkness, starved down to the bone. I couldn't bear to watch how ... I knew I wouldn't have the time to take care of him, to say nothing of the money. Perhaps I didn't give him enough exercise. Perhaps he simply had surplus energy ..."

"Now the whole guilt business is starting again," Valerie

said. "That isn't why I've come. Let's not talk about that. There is no point."

The horse came a few paces closer and stopped about three yards away. Korbas was anything but beautiful. His ribs poked out of his flanks, his head was enormous, his eyes were watering, his neck was long and thin, making him look rather like a giraffe. There was about him none of that beauty one expects from an animal which normally personifies beauty and grace. And that's the sort of horse Miriam loved, thought Valerie, and once again she was impressed by her twelve-year-old daughter's generosity of heart.

The horse's eyes had such a sad look that what Valerie would have liked most of all was to lay her arms round his neck and weep.

"I'm glad I've come," she said.

"He's a pitiable creature," Alexander Hausch answered. "I don't know whether he's ever had anything good in his life. Presumably even as a foal he was contemptibly punished because he's so ugly and shapeless. Yet nobody was decisive enough to turn him into horse meat."

Korbas seemed to notice that he was being talked about because his expression became even sadder. His overlarge skull hung down like a log as if about to fall off at any moment.

"The only good thing he had ever had was Miriam. She loved him. She treated him like a king, brushed him, plaited his mane, lunged him, fed him carrots, for her he was the most beautiful horse and whenever anybody made nasty comments about him she defended him to the last." He gave a deep sigh. "I simply can't grasp it. Sometimes I think the earth was created just to torture innocent creatures."

"Somebody told me that you were here when it happened."

"I was here ..."

"How ...?"

Alexander Hausch took a deep breath. "It was totally banal. A really windy day. This lorry drove past the riding paddock a good fifty yards away, it was loaded with hay covered by a blue plastic sheet ... and suddenly this blue sheet came flying over. I can still remember thinking: I don't believe it. Miriam was with Korbas on the paddock and the sheet was soaring directly towards them. I thought: for the love of god, what a nightmare. All I saw was confusion, Korbas is terrified of plastic sheets, he must have shied ... when the sheet went flapping away, Miriam was lying on the ground and Korbas was standing next to her. I couldn't see anything but they ascertained that his hoof must have shattered her skull. Forgive me, I shouldn't have mentioned that."

"Yes, you should."

Korbas came closer now and stopped right in front of Valerie. To have him so close aroused in her a flood of feelings which were very hard to bear. Fury, numbness. But how could she blame the horse, this poor, miserable creature?

Given the way he looked she had to ask herself who was suffering most, him or her.

"He misses her," said Alexander Hausch. "Since she has been gone, nothing can rouse him. It breaks my heart whenever I come to the stable."

"Poor thing," Valerie murmured.

Alexander Hausch chewed at his lower lip. "It may seem grotesque to you that I'm an insurance agent and yet have no personal liability insurance for the horse."

Valerie looked at him in astonishment. "What use would that be to me?"

"You have every right to take me to court."

"You mean I could get rich on it?" she asked.

"Well, if I had the money ..."

Valerie was plunged into an internal emptiness out of which tiny white feathers seemed to be rising. Korbas came even closer and the two empty eyes in his bony skull were right in front of hers. She imagined him as a foal gambling across the field, drinking from his mother and looking out into the world full of hope. Suddenly in those sad eyes dancing lights appeared, a waterfall in all the colours of the rainbow. She felt exactly how much happiness Miriam had given this horse and how happy he had made her. Two souls who had found one another. And now Miriam was gone and would never return.

"He cannot grasp why she's no longer here," Valerie said.

"He mourns for her," said Hausch. "You should have seen the two of them together. I have never known a human being and a horse thrive so well with each other. He hardly eats anything anymore. If it goes on like this, he'll die."

"Thank you, Mr Hausch."

"I'm so sorry," he said and wiped a tear from his eye. "I'd simply reached my financial limits. For twenty years I've had horses that were always insured. Somehow, I thought, nothing would happen with this good-natured soul."

"I don't want money," replied Valerie. "Money would not console me. Even less so if Miriam's death were to ruin you. I'm glad I came. I'm happy I was able to meet Korbas."

"I hope I can find somebody to take care of him. I have two other horses and a full-time job. You don't perhaps...?"

"Know anybody? I'm not acquainted with horse people. I was always afraid of horses and I've never really felt drawn to them," Valerie replied.

"It's perhaps presumptuous of me but I was wondering whether you ... "

"Me?" replied Valerie astonished. "No, that's ... I know

nothing about horses."

"You could learn."

"I ..." She looked at the large brown horse. "No, I couldn't. I sympathize with him and I'm sorry that, like me, he has lost Miriam but I don't have what's needed to take on the responsibility for such an animal."

"I would go on paying the stable fees, pay for the food and the farrier. The vet's fees. All you would have to do would be to come and ... I'll show you how to lunge him, how to lift his hooves and, if you wish, also how to ride." Alexander Hausch seemed to be inspired by the idea.

"No, it's not possible."

"Sorry I asked. I'd forgotten what you're going through."

"I understand you but I am definitely not the right person."

"Of course, of course." He patted the sad horse and Valerie went back to her car.

20

Miou behaved as if she had never known Valerie.

"My dear Miou. I missed you." The velvety-eyed cat pushed herself through the slightly open door between the hall and the living room and dashed off. She's mad at me because I've left her alone for so long, Valerie reasoned.

She had taken a taxi home from the airport, had simply dumped her bag down and rushed straight off to the stable. She had phoned Alexander Hausch from the Atlanta airport after she had found his insurance office website on the Internet and had made an appointment with him. She had considered it important to meet him before she got caught up again in the realities of Schlattstall.

Now Valerie unpacked her bag, took her boots out of the plastic carrier and found that on the soles there was still dust and dirt from the ranch. She had brought a bunch of dried sage with her which she wanted to save for an important moment that she knew was approaching although as yet she did not know what it would look like.

Tremendous longing to see Gitanes again overwhelmed her but she loathed the idea of meeting Evi.

The supply of cat food was used up and if she wanted to make it to the shops she had to go. She had almost completely emptied her travelling bag, there was just one side pocket left. And there she found her road map of Arizona and a bundle wrapped in cloth. She unwrapped it and a hand-sized, decorative horseshoe emerged. With it was a torn off piece of paper with a handwritten note, which read: "Someone is waiting for this." Valerie smirked. She was almost a 100 per cent sure that Salik had smuggled it into the luggage. A greeting from a world that seemed to be a dream but without any doubt it actually existed.

Valerie put the souvenir in her jacket pocket and grabbed the car keys. After all, horseshoes were lucky.

Evi received her with the words: "I thought you'd have come sooner."

"I've brought something for you," Valerie replied.

Evi felt the horseshoe and sighed deeply the way she did whenever she received a message from fellow souls. Valerie wondered whether Evi actually knew that a woman like Salik Noor had bought this horseshoe, perhaps even intending it for Evi. Anything was possible, Valerie thought.

"That's very kind," Evi said. "You seem to have met a few interesting people there."

Valerie was on the point of relating something about her journey—two or three sentences—but she felt that Evi was in a bad mood, that she was probably still sore about their argument last time, which was understandable after all, or perhaps it was just one of her usual mood swings.

"How are the horses?" Valerie asked.

"Gitanes is fine even though he is gradually preparing himself for his departure."

Valerie's heart clenched: "What departure?"

She stormed out onto the terrace. He was standing at the other end of the paddock. Her longing for him became unbearable as if all the wonderful, mysterious things that she had experienced would evaporate if he was no longer there. All the things she had experienced were very concrete in her imagination yet also very far removed from her world in Germany and she did not know how to combine the two worlds without him. He was the bridge.

Gitanes turned his head to her without really making contact and went on grazing. Valerie felt she was walking on thin ice and could easily fall through. Evi stood at her back and Valerie felt a surge of animosity blowing against her from behind. She realized that she first had to sort things out with Evi.

"I'm sorry about all the things I said last time and I want to apologize," Valerie said.

"That's not the point."

"What *is* the point then?" Valerie asked.

"I just can't bear your self-righteousness."

"I can't see where I am self-righteous when all I feel is grief and pain ... and ... I don't know ..."

"You and your pain, you're world champions."

"All I want is to see Gitanes. Please let me be alone with him for a while. Then I'll go again. I'll go to the mill and get you the horse muesli that you like so much."

"Gitanes doesn't want to see you."

"I don't see why you ... what you have against me."

"You can't bear me either."

Valerie laughed. "But by some coincidence my medicine horse is here in your field. I must see him even if it means defeating Cerberus, the hound of hell, to get there."

"Cerberus, the hell hound, am I really that bad?"

Evi appeared to think it over quite seriously. "I'm sorry about that."

Evi's expression became unexpectedly mild: "It just makes me mad that you are so blind."

"I'm blind? But why? ... I experienced so many things in Arizona."

"That's just it, you know but you don't act."

"What do I know and what in your opinion should I do?"

Evi sighed, this time not because the spirits were talking

to her but because something was frustrating her intensely.

Gitanes raised his head and came trotting up to Evi, the pressure in Valerie's chest eased. Gitanes snuggled against Evi and immediately her anger and frustration ebbed away, Evi's face was suddenly beautiful, gracious. Valerie had never before seen this beauty in her.

Oh Gitanes, Valerie thought, you simply know what to do, don't you?

"What do you mean by 'blind'?" Valerie asked again. "Really, I'm quite open. If there's something I can't see ... I'll fully accept that, so please, tell me."

"It's not about Gitanes," Evi said.

"Who is it about then?"

"Korbas."

What made her think of him?

"You visited him this afternoon."

"How do you know that?"

"Because he told me," Evi said drily.

Valerie swallowed. "And why Korbas?"

"He needs you."

Now Valerie sighed—from the very bottom of her heart. In one stroke it became clear to her that Evi belonged to these fanatical animal protectors who expected their fellow beings to sacrifice themselves in order to look after these poor creatures, who anyway had long decided that earthly existence was not for them.

"I won't take on the responsibility of Korbas," Valerie said harshly.

"Because he's ugly?"

Valerie felt herself getting angry. This Evi woman managed it every time. She didn't want to have to justify to Evi that she was not born a horse owner.

"Because you think he killed your daughter?"

"For one thing. How can you expect me to take into my

life a horse that will always remind me of that?"

Evi snorted like a horse releasing tension. "I would have expected rather more courage from you."

"I don't understand." Valerie felt paralyzed. She was sick of it. The whole thing was so incredibly difficult.

"Why will nobody help me? I just can't do it," Valerie said. She would have much preferred to go, to leave Evi and Gitanes and everything else behind her, simply slip into some strange, unknown person's skin and start a new life. Certainly, she had experienced impressive things in Arizona, she had gained a glimpse into the web of reality, had felt Miriam's incredible love, and now understood that she was not responsible for her death. But this earthly world still felt miserable, her grief was still strong, and new problems and disagreements kept on emerging.

As if to confirm this the paint horse produced a heap of horse apples.

"I'll go," Valerie said. "I can't take on the care of a horse. I need care myself."

Evi looked at her blankly.

Valerie ground her teeth. "I'm afraid I am blind and egotistic, I'm limited and do not have a halo."

She headed for the terrace door and Evi followed her.

"Where's Tom?"

Valerie stopped dead.

"Just ask him yourself. I'm sure he'll answer you—from the Arizona desert, even without mobile phone reception."

Valerie sat down on the sofa in her living room, weeping, the daffodils blossoming outside caught her eye. The sight of them triggered another outbreak of tears. Miou clambered onto her lap and curled up.

"Evi is head over heels in love with Tom, she hates me because she thinks I flirt with him but I don't want anything from him. Don't want anything from anybody ... I thought I had overcome my grief and every other possible problem, too, but now I'm back here and I still can't get over the fact that Miriam is no longer here, and I start arguments with people who mean me no harm, who actually just want to give me a kick up the backside so that I finally wake up." Involuntarily she thought of Korbas, that horrible, poor creature standing alone in his stable with nobody to love him.

The telephone rang. From the display she saw that it was Tamara. 'For god's sake don't answer' went through her mind, then as if in a trance, she reached for the receiver.

"Hello."

"How was it?"

Dodging the question Valerie said: "Fine ... How are you?"

"Oh well, ... it's difficult with Mark again."

Huh, Valerie thought, sometimes it has its advantages when other people aren't that interested in you. Bitching about Mark, Valerie thought, would improve her mood.

"Hm, not exactly easy?" Valerie said. "Up to now that's what you liked about him."

Valerie noticed that the answer was a trace too provocative for Tamara.

"He's not that bad," Tamara said pointedly.

Valerie asked: "Did you have another nice spin in his Porsche?"

"Not exactly. He's possessed by the thought of finding that horse that killed Miriam—and shooting it. He's got a gun permit ..."

Valerie flinched as if somebody had touched her skull with a tuning fork to produce a particular, revealing sound.

"What the hell's made him suddenly think of that?"

"He's already mentioned it. Don't you remember Rita's

birthday?"

"The horse is none of his damn business."

"Men are simply like that ... I know he was never interested in Miriam. Always thought she was a bit disturbed ... but she's family and he's got a strong sense of family loyalty and a sense of justice second to none. There is a hunter in him, you know ... an avenger. I believe there's an avenger in every real man, after all that's how we've survived for five million years."

Valerie's thoughts rolled with provocative speed along a riverbed. "I don't quite understand ... What is he up to?"

"As I've said, he wants to shoot the horse."

"But he doesn't even know it. He doesn't even know where to find it or what its name is. He'll end up shooting the wrong one."

"He'll find out."

"This is all totally absurd."

"It is. Sometimes he's just crazy, but I had to tell you."

"How are Tom and Rita?" Valerie asked, trying to gain a breath of relief.

"Good. Very good," Tamara replied. "One of the dogs gobbled up Mum's liquor chocolates and now they want to have a kennel built."

Valerie laughed without being able to say exactly why. In any case this was exactly the reality she had been afraid of returning to. A reality that was eons away from the light and love she had experienced in Arizona. Yet also a reality that was hard to escape.

A crazy thought shot through her head. "You know what, I'm just wondering whether *I* should perhaps murder *Mark*. Then we'd all have one problem less."

"What are you talking about?" Tamara answered curtly. "I don't need you to take the piss ... Can do that myself."

"No, I really mean it."

Valerie was determined to pursue any line that would lead away from repeating the same old, absurd conversation she always had with her sister.

"Hey, what's up with you? I thought you'd been researching cactuses. You sound as if you'd swallowed LSD or drunk *ayahuasca*. Isn't that brewed from cactuses?"

"Neither nor," Valerie said and laughed out loud. "And what I said about Mark I mean quite seriously. If he lays one finger on that horse, I'll personally come over and blow his brains out."

As soon as she had fired off this sentence, she cut the conversation dead—leaving Tamara no chance to answer.

21

I'm floating in a vacuum, was Valerie's first thought when she woke up the next morning. Miou was standing with her front paws on Valerie's chest and poking her nose into her face, she was hungry. It occurred to Valerie that she hadn't brought the promised postcard for her neighbour, Mrs Retter, who had fed Miou, and also that she had forgotten to buy cat food the day before.

I must see a horse, she thought, as she scratched the remaining fish paste into Miou's dish and crammed a piece of frozen bread into the slit of the toaster. I have to get my feet back on the ground. *I have to go to Gitanes,* my medicine horse.

She parked her car about a hundred yards from Evi's overgrown residence, round a bend so that Evi would not notice she was coming, unless whispering spirits gave her away—and Valerie had seen to that by sending up an urgent prayer to whoever-was-up-there. She had to commune with Gitanes alone, Evi's presence would only produce too much atmospheric disturbance.

Valerie plunged through the dense undergrowth to the other end of the field and sat down between two hazelnut bushes, where she could not be seen. Gitanes, though, had seen her.

"Come here to me, medicine horse," she murmured. He

flicked his ears quietly, attentively, as if he wanted to send her an invisible message through the ether. Valerie wondered whether Evi might be looking through the kitchen window and could tell by the horse's behaviour that there was a human being nearby. Valerie's thoughts drifted away and became entangled in all sorts of different scenarios … Gitanes turned back to the grass. Valerie's courage dropped like a stone into a deep shaft. Gitanes had lost his respect for her. Why should a proud, beautiful horse be interested in somebody who had been summoned by Chief Black Falcon to a journey into the beyond, to the world of spirits— but had now come back to earth so miserably, having learnt nothing?

"You have to help me, old fellow. I'm lost, I'm hovering weightlessly back and forth between the worlds. I was at this ceremony," she began. "I saw Miriam again and Tom was a … guardian angel. Did I just imagine all that? Where is Miriam? Or is none of that important? Must I really just return to my old life after all that, to work and forget?"

Three ants crawled across her hand and proceeded up her sleeve. When she tried to shake them off, her arm dipped into a clump of stinging nettles. Ouch, that'll hurt. When she looked up she saw that Gitanes had come to within two paces of the fence.

"So you have come," she whispered. Again he raised his head and listened as if he could hear something. This time Valerie did not think of Evi and realized that things went better when she did not think of her.

Valerie sat upright and let her soul plunge into the large, black-and-white-dappled body like a stone into a deep pond. There she felt herself supported. She now felt that Gitanes was with her. She hugged her knees and let her head fall forwards. She felt her consciousness shift and suddenly there was a waft from the world she had experienced in Arizona.

"I thank you, medicine horse," she said. "I knew you would understand me." Gitanes lifted his head and turned his gaze into the distance, proud and wise.

"That business with Mark, do you think I have to take it seriously? Korbas, poor unhappy soul ... I don't understand why Mark is so angry with him. What a complete idiot." She plucked a stalk of grass and stroked her nose with it. Gitanes' jaws chomped. With the long, thin grass stalk Valerie stroked her hand, turned it over and looked at her palm. When she saw a spider sitting there she laughed.

"The whole thing seems to me strangely interwoven," she said and in the context of the spider found her choice of words really clairvoyant. "Like an equation that I can't solve. Do you understand that, medicine horse?" Gitanes looked at her attentively. "I only feel how this strange web, these strange interlacings, are more and more finely spun ... apparently, it seems to me, until I have understood why ... Not with my reason, it can't be understood at all with reason."

She looked at Gitanes and in the expression on his face she suddenly saw Miriam.

A knot was tightening in her stomach. "What are you trying to tell me?"

"There is something there that I'm not seeing, something that's hidden—why?" Gitanes turned and ran to the other end of the field. Normally she would now have been sad or perhaps offended, but this time she did not feel rejected, she felt suffused with warm feelings. Gentleness spread like warm fire in her chest. The sun emerged from behind the clouds and warmed her cheeks. Valerie closed her eyes.

She was finally learning to understand what had connected Miriam to animals. There was no great secret about it. Valerie remembered how, as a girl, she had danced with the poppies and had exchanged secrets with butterflies.

If Miriam's Light Body—as had been her impression in Arizona—could determine her fate, why then had she gone? Because of me? Because she did not feel at home with me? Because I had forgotten this beautiful place where animals and humans intermingle? No. Miriam knows that deep within myself I am still like that—and always was. She liked being with me. She felt my love. I know that. Thank you, ants and nettles, thank you, dear spider, thank you, Gitanes, thank you all for reminding me.

Gitanes was standing at the other end of the field and was still looking into the distance as if he was pursuing some important thought.

He too is leaving me, Valerie thought. Evi is right. He will go. From the very beginning it was as if he would only be here for a limited time. It's OK, Valerie thought. Something else will turn up.

She bent slightly forwards and saw that Evi was standing on the terrace. So she did get wind of it, Valerie thought. But she had found what she had been looking for, she was now ready to meet Evi without reservation.

When Valerie reached the terrace, she saw Evi on the swing fixed to a cross beam, she was pushing herself off with her foot and swung quietly backwards and forwards. She seemed to be in a placid mood. Valerie leant against one of the wooden veranda posts and noticed that there was a sign scratched on it, a four-part circle with segments coloured in with chalk: red, black, blue, white.

"I still can't see the whole picture but I now understand what you mean by my being blind," Valerie said.

"In a fragile moment everything can change. Each breath can change everything. Everything depends on how you act—and when," Evi said through the squeaking of the swing.

Valerie's stomach clenched. Not in answer to what Evi had said but in response to something that came flying out of the air and settled. Out of the blue Gitanes suddenly leapt aside and galloped off across the field. He turned and galloped back with his head thrown back, stopped, hesitated then hurtled off again.

"What's wrong with him?" Valerie asked astonished. Now he was running towards her and stopped just a few paces away. He looked at her with his large, gentle eyes.

Valerie turned searchingly to Evi. "Tell me! What's wrong?"

Evi's expression remained impassive.

Then Valerie understood. She ran off to her car, slammed the door and turned the key. She still did not know where she had to go but she would find out.

22

As if she were in some thriller being pursued by the Mafia, Valerie careened down the tortuous road in her little car. At the same time she tried to keep her psychic channels open, so that intuitions could fly in like butterflies. In a steep bend she veered into the on-coming lane and at that very moment a black BMW came hurtling head-on towards her. The driver blasted his horn at her furiously. Horrified Valerie wrenched the steering wheel round and collided with the steep rock face, shattering the off-side mirror, the car went into a skid …

The steering wheel shuddered in her hands until finally she got the car under control again. Trembling all over she stopped by the roadside. It's not a good idea to try telepathic communication while driving, she thought, at least not when you take a sharp bend at 75mph.

With a more appropriate speed of 25 she crawled on.

In Unterlenningen the road was closed for repairs. She turned into the road marked DIVERSION. A mile or so further on she found herself confronted by a dung heap on a large farm. She must have overlooked some sign or other.

She wept with frustration. 'What am I doing here? I've flipped my lid and nearly killed both myself and another driver.' She drove forward a few yards to get out of sight of the houses and turned off the engine. She leant forwards, supporting her head on the steering wheel and tried to breathe calmly.

Again she had the feeling that at this very moment something odd was happening and that she had to do something about it. But her mind was blank.

She sighed and closed her eyes. I couldn't prevent Miriam's death either, although I must have had some subconscious inkling, at least if I am to believe what Tom said about having already sent Gitanes to Evi's last summer. I'm so blind!

At last. At last. Valerie turned the ignition key. That's what it feels like when you *know* something, the way Evi *knew* things, the way Tom or Salik *knew* something ...

She turned and drove back the way she had come till she found the diversion sign she had overlooked. Her mobile phone rang.

"You have to help me!" Tamara shouted in panic. "Mark has found the horse, he's on his way there."

"Me, too," Valerie replied.

Mark's Porsche stood in front of the barn. Valerie saw him talking to the farm-owner who was pointing in the direction of the paddock. Valerie recognized the skeletal animal with the brown coat, the formless figure of Korbas, who stood out from the other grazing horses. He was standing apart under an apple tree. Mark would not shoot the horse in broad daylight. Could he be so insane? Yes, he could, Valerie answered. She saw him dip his hand into the pocket of his bomber jacket and run off. Did he have the gun there in his jacket pocket? The farmer, in rubber boots, suspected nothing and climbed back up onto his tractor.

"Mark!" Valerie screamed.

Mark turned as he ran, recognized her but kept running. The horses raised their heads.

"He's got a gun," Valerie shouted to the farmer. "He's going to kill him, kill Korbas."

The man looked at Valerie, dumbfounded and glanced at Mark, then he scuttled back down off the tractor.

Mark positioned himself at the fence, took the weapon out of his pocket and aimed.

With great presence of mind Valerie bent down for a stone and aimed too. "I'll save you, Korbas," she whispered. "And now get out of the firing line." Then she threw the stone at the horse as hard as she could. It must have struck him a fraction of a second earlier than the bullet would have, because he jumped to one side and was unharmed.

Mark aimed again.

"Run, Korbas!" Valerie screamed. She saw a lunge whip propped against the stable wall, grabbed it by the long, thin handle, slipped through the fence and ran towards the herd, swinging the whip. She was aware of moving into Mark's range but he would not kill her. And if he did ...

The horses scattered away from the whip in all directions. Valerie concentrated on Korbas. As long as he was moving, Mark would find it hard to hit him. She made sure she kept between Mark and Korbas, acting as a protective shield.

In the meantime the farmer had reached Mark. Out of the corner of her eye Valerie saw him throw himself at Mark and knock the gun from his hand. As a former policeman Mark was in good condition, he knocked the powerful farmer to the ground.

Valerie felt helpless.

She saw her sister's silver Audi turn into the farm, watched Tamara hurrying across the yard.

"Mark, stop!" Tamara screamed. He turned towards her. His expression froze. It went through Valerie's head: he will kill her. And in fact Mark bent down and picked the gun up from the ground.

"Stupid cow. What are you talking about?" Mark yelled at Tamara.

"I'm your wife, Mark," came Tamara's answer in a quivering voice. "Give me the gun..."

She walked towards him.

"You stay there!" Mark bellowed.

Tamara obeyed.

"It's not the horse's fault," she said. Valerie had to admire her sister's courage.

"It killed your niece—and you want it to survive? Because it's an animal? Does it have a right to go on living? Who allows me to live? I hate these animal activists. They see to it that such killers run around free."

Again he stepped to the fence and aimed at Korbas.

"Mark, please ..."

Mark's hand swung from Korbas to Tamara. The barrel of the gun was aimed at her head.

Valerie was scared to death.

"Tell me you want the animal to live."

"It makes no sense, Mark."

Mark would not be pacified.

"Either the horse dies or you do," he said. "It's your choice."

"Mark, I beg you."

"You think I'm just joking."

"No."

A shot split the air. Valerie saw her sister flinch.

"I'm waiting for your answer."

"Take me then," Tamara said.

Mark stood there, indecisive, then he lowered the gun, went to her, grabbed her by the arm and dragged her to his Porsche. They got in and drove off.

Valerie was still shaking all over.

The whip lay on the ground. The large brown horse came up to her and thrust his enormous, bony head in her face. He blew warm air from his nostrils. The smell produced a memory of the dog which had lived in their neighbourhood when she was small, she had always stroked him and afterwards had smelled her hands.

She reached out and touched Korbas' neck. His eyes bore a gentle expression. The fear, the terror of the last few moments fell away as if he were absorbing them into his huge body.

Valerie sat down under one of the apple trees. Korbas came and snuffled at her. Then he turned to graze very close to her.

Valerie surrendered to the currents of her feelings. It seemed to her that her Arizona experiences had only just reached her. Everything intermingled: what had happened in Arizona, what had just happened and what was still happening. She had adopted him. He was her horse now, there was no way back. "You've managed that very cleverly, big brown brute," she said.

Her mobile rang.
"Everything OK?" It was Evi.
"Yes."
"Gitanes was most disturbed and I was worried."
"Everything is OK."
Valerie told Evi what had happened and ended by saying: "I have the feeling that everything is fine now."
"What about your sister?"
"I hope she'll slowly understand that he's a killer and will be strong enough to boot him up the arse."
Evi laughed. "Be careful with your prophecies."
"OK," Valerie replied.
"Miriam is still here," she said after a while.

"I think she has stayed this long, so I'll look after Korbas. I'll phone Alexander Hausch later and ask him to transfer the papers to me. Then perhaps I can let Miriam go in peace."

23

Back home Valerie washed her hands and popped a deep-frozen pizza into the oven, then she dialed her sister Tamara's mobile number. Tamara was on her way to a woman-friend's in Lübeck. She had reported Mark to the police because of repeated physical and psychological violence. She had also informed her lawyer. For the coming weeks she would hide from Mark with this friend.

"I'm sorry that he directed his anger at the horse of all things. I don't understand why."

Valerie wanted to explain to Tamara something about fields mutually attracting each other and triggering reciprocal events, but she was too confused herself and could not find the right words to convey something so mysterious.

"How are you?" Tamara asked and this time her interest sounded genuine.

"I'm now a horse owner."

"Congratulations. That suits you."

"Suits me?" Valerie could hardly believe it.

"You always had that side to you. And now your superbrain will calm down a bit."

"I haven't a clue about horses. Tomorrow morning I have to turn up to muck out the stable."

"That sounds like fun."

That night Valerie slept restlessly, Miou was not lying at her feet as she usually did. She often stayed away overnight but tonight of all nights Valerie would have liked to have her there. But then, after all, it was her own fault because she still had not managed to get cat food and there was only dry stuff left. Surely Miou got better treatment with the neighbour, Mrs Retter. Valerie dreamt of Miriam and when she woke up the next morning she had the feeling that Miriam's spirit had left the flat. But she also knew that her spirit was still present in the earthly world.

With a piece of jam toast in her hand Valerie went into her daughter's room, stopped in the middle and looked around. Perhaps I should throw some things away.

She took the postcard with the black-and-white paint horse from the drawer. She thought of Tom, he had wanted to stay in Arizona for a few more days but he ought to be back by now. Valerie dialed his mobile number.

"I got back yesterday," Tom said, "I'm supposed to deliver greetings from Salik and the others. They hope you'll come back."

Valerie wanted to tell him about the latest events but he already knew everything from Evi.

"Evi said Gitanes will be going away."

"I have rented a farm near Nuremberg. I'll be moving there with Gitanes. Evi will be coming, too," he said.

Were they a couple after all? No, she could not imagine that. But who knows? On the other hand, just because people lived together that did not immediately make them a couple. Perhaps they just wanted to work more closely together in the future. Valerie found it painful that she would lose Evi and Tom after they had only just become her friends. But she would not worry about that now. After all she could always go and visit Tom and Evi ... and Gitanes.

"You are one of us now," Tom said.

"I'm a beginner," Valerie replied. Then she added: "Or perhaps you could say: newly initiated."

"In a very powerful way," Tom answered.

Valerie felt a waft of the Arizona experiences. "I have the feeling it's as if right now they are all here: Salik, Karma, Chuck, Derek … ."

"They're always here."

Valerie was silent. She felt an intense bond with Tom, with the companions from Arizona—the members of her tribe—as Tom called them.

"May I ask you another question, Tom?"

"Sure."

"I have the feeling that Miriam's spirit is still here. What can I do so that she can finally go?"

"Give me a few moments," Tom replied.

Valerie imagined him consulting his spirit guides. He cleared his throat as if he had found the answer. "It was planned for her to take an animal with her. But that's changed now," Tom said.

"Korbas?" Valerie asked. "He was supposed to die? … And I prevented it. What does that mean?"

"In a certain way she seems to think that you have not quite understood the message."

Valerie was confused. "But I have agreed to look after Korbas. What can she still be thinking?"

"I don't know," Tom said. "You'll see."

"So long, Tom."

Valerie put down the receiver and looked at the postcard in her hand. She put it back in the drawer. There was more involved than throwing away a postcard. It occurred to her that she had a horse to look after. On her way to the stable she would stop at the supermarket, get some cat food and stock up with supplies. She made an appointment with Alexander Hausch to deal with the papers for Korbas and she had to make a contract with Mr. Starke, the farm owner, to be able to keep the horse there. Where was Miou?

It was dark when Valerie got home from the stable and the supermarket. She carried the bag of shopping in and put it down on the kitchen counter. She had never felt such a strange mood in the flat before. The room was both empty and full at the same time. Miou was still missing and Miriam's spirit seemed to have returned. It seemed to be hovering in the rooms as if at any moment Miriam would emerge from a cloud of mist and stand there before her. The wooden cupboard creaked as if it was about to fall apart. Usually Miou was always here when she came home, she made a game of waiting at the front door till Valerie came back.

"Do you perhaps know where my cat is?"

"Yes," Mrs Retter said. She looked as if she had shrunk even more since the last time Valerie had seen her. When she looked Mrs Retter in the eye, Valerie had an ominous feeling. Mrs Retter lifted her arm like a gnarled branch and invited Valerie in. Stale air and the odours of furniture which presumably had been standing around for a hundred of years enveloped her. Valerie went weak in the knees.

I have acquired the ability to sense misfortune, she thought, and with the next breath she knew what had happened.

Repeatedly Mrs Retter tried in vain to open a creaking drawer, Valerie wanted to offer her help, but she felt too weak. At last Mrs Retter managed to get the drawer open wide enough for her to take out a torch.

The light streaming from the living room only lit half the garden, Mrs Retter used the torch to illuminate the other half. Between the tulips and the daffodils there was a blank area a couple of feet square. There in the ground stood a metal cross with a figure of Christ. A ring of flowers was draped round the cross—in the shape of a heart.

"She was run over."

"When?"

"Yesterday afternoon. I was doing some weeding behind the house. The front door was open, Miou was with me, she had come to visit. I heard the screech of brakes. I ran round into the street ... and there she lay. She was dead on the spot."

"Miou," ... Valerie felt her legs giving way. "Miou ..."

"I'm very sorry," Mrs Retter said. "I carried her into the garden. Then I thought that it's not good for you to see the dead cat having just lost your child. I thought it would be better if I made a nice grave for her—I'm really so sorry."

Tears flowed down Valerie's cheeks into the corners of her mouth. She was glad that Mrs Retter did not blame anybody: not the driver, nor her, Valerie—nor herself. It felt good to just stand here and say nothing.

Valerie felt deep gratitude to Miou for having been her faithful companion for so many years and finally, after Miriam's death, her only friend. Valerie had a feeling of standing within some mystery, a vibrating space in the centre of which a door opened through which she watched Miou pass.

"I'm sorry I must go. Thank you, Mrs Retter. Thank you very much."

"I would like to tell you something else, Mrs Rosenstein, even if I don't know you very well." Mrs Retter's voice became especially soft. "When Miou visited me, I often talked to her. It may sound strange to you that an old woman should talk to a cat."

"No, no."

"Miou knew she was going to die on the same day you came back from America. She told me."

They were standing silently at the grave. "Thank you for telling me that."

"I would like to ask you to keep this conversation to yourself. People here in the village would consider me insane, and I have to get on with these people for the rest of my life," Mrs Retter said.

"That's all the more reason to thank you for your trust," Valerie said. "And for everything else that you did for Miou. I'm sorry I forgot to bring you back the postcard that I promised. But perhaps you'll have some time in the next few days for me to tell you about Arizona."

"Yes, that would be nice."

Valerie knelt down by the grave. "Oh Miou, you great soul. How rich am I to have had you in my life. How gentle is your spirit, how great your wisdom. May my tears accompany you across the river into the other world. There's one more thing left to do—and I will accomplish it."

24

Light shimmered through the leaves of the horse chestnut into Evi's living room. Valerie was relieved that Evi was at home. She remembered that to start with she had thought Evi very weird, but in the meantime she had got to know her better and usually could even understand her now. Today Evi seemed unusually cheerful and clear.

"I'd like to ask you to carry out a ceremony with me in which I can say good-bye to Miriam and Miou," Valerie said.

Evi nodded as if she had already expected something of the kind.

Valerie sat down on the sofa, with her knees together and her hands clamped between them. I hope I'm ready, she thought. A knot was forming in her stomach.

Evi disappeared and returned after a while in a long, red skirt with bones and feathers attached to it. Over it she was wearing a white, long-sleeved shirt with a black, fringed stole round her shoulders. From a thin silver chain round her neck hung a medallion in the form of a coiled snake.

"Come on," she said and led Valerie down the hall to a room Valerie had not seen before.

Two wall lamps shed sparse light. At one end of the room there was an altar on which there stood the statue of a dark-skinned Madonna in a blue dress. Evi set up three large candles: white, red and black.

"The white one stands for Miriam, the black for Miou and the red one for you," Evi said. She handed Valerie a fourth, thin, white candle and asked her to light them.

"Ask the souls of the three to show their light."

Valerie lit the candles. The white one, standing for Miriam, flickered like a will-o'-the-wisp, Miou's burnt calmly. It felt strange to be lighting a candle for her own soul but it was not unpleasant. Just a few weeks before she would have dismissed all this as hocus-pocus and she certainly wouldn't have been seen dead in such a situation, yet now it seemed to her appropriate—more than that: the procedure had a sacred beauty all of its own.

"Next I want you to kneel down at the altar," Evi said.

Valerie felt a brief inner resistance to this request, then she acquiesced.

Evi started a chant which sounded like a mixture of Indian chanting, Hawaiian folk dance and a Turkish pop song. Suddenly Valerie felt quite clearly the presence of Miriam and Miou. She also felt Gitanes' spirit und when she looked at the brown cloth that was draped over the altar she recognized in the black forms scrawled on it the outlines of Korbas. The room was filled with supportive spirits. A wave of sadness swept over Valerie, then she was gripped by indistinct reverence. The feeling was replaced by astonishment that she was actually in the presence of all these souls and that they had come to be at her side.

"Are you ready?" Evi asked.

"Yes, I am ready," Valerie replied.

"Direct your eyes to the three candles. I will make contact with the two souls. You will be able to tell which one is addressing you, your eyes will turn there by themselves."

Valerie had expected something dramatic: a ritual with swathes of incense, vibrating tables and flickering lights.

But in fact everything happened in complete silence. Without her intervention her gaze wandered to the black candle. She saw Miou before her inner eye, not in her physical form but in the form of her soul.

"She is so old," Valerie said. "Ancient." She did not know where the certainty came from that Miou had already lived many lives. As a cat, as a falcon, as an animal now extinct that Valerie had seen in a book about ancient history. A bison, a breed of cattle with a shaggy coat and long, curved horns. She saw these animals although they were not there physically. She did not really see them, their clear outlines, it was more an awareness, certainty that they were present.

"Was your death coincidence?" Valerie asked the spirit of the cat.

The answer came: I'm too old for coincidences.

"But what did it mean then?"

Involuntarily Valerie's eyes turned to the white candle standing for Miriam. Now she saw the two souls—that of the girl and that of the cat—united as if they were embracing like two friends who do everything together, wear the same T-shirts and also die together.

We belong together, the cat said.

"And me?" Pain shot through Valerie. Her gaze was now directed at the red candle, her own. "Why do I stay behind, alone?" Loneliness lay like a heavy blanket round her shoulders. "Now there is no other soul to be with me, to accompany me."

This time the spirits remained silent. The pain grew, it spread in her limbs like fire, filling her completely. There was something about this pain that was different from the stifling feelings which since Miriam's death had sucked all the life out of her. This pain did not remain fixed, it buried itself deep as if it were looking for the end of the tunnel, seeking an exit into the light. While this pain was working within her, Valerie felt somewhere beyond her control a breath of salvation. The pain had not come to torture her further, it had come to heal her.

Valerie heard Evi's voice saying: "Would you like to lie down?" She turned round and saw that Evi had laid out a thick woollen blanket on the floor. A falcon with out-stretched wings was depicted on it.

"Oh yes." Valerie felt as heavy as lead. She had just enough strength to sink slowly to her knees.

"I'm so frightened of being alone, without Miriam, without Miou. The loneliness is so overwhelming."

A spade dug into the earth of her body. It struck a sub-terranean water vein, a few drops seeped up through the earth. A tear trickled from Valerie's eyes, then two, then three. More and more streams surged up through the earth. As if a spring had forced its way to the surface.

As she wept, Miriam and Miou were there with her in a way she had never felt when they were both still alive. What Valerie now felt was the pure essence of these twin souls. She was not alone. Miou and Miriam were with her. That provided consolation but, at the same time, pain, for she knew that she must bid farewell to them both. They had been so close to her when they were alive and that was why she could hardly bear to let them go. And yet she felt for the first time that she was equal to the task.

"I am ready," Valerie said to Evi in a quivering voice.

"Blow out the white and the black candles," Evi said.

Valerie sensed what this meant. "I thereby allow them to go."

"Yes."

"It's the natural course of things, isn't it?"

"You alone know the answer, Valerie."

"Yes, I know it."

Valerie got up.

"I thank you, Miou, for touching my soul. May you bless many others in the same way." She bent forwards, breathing out quietly. The light flickered as if it were putting up some final resistance, then the flame went out. Valerie clearly felt Miou's spirit leave the room.

The second task required more energy. This was not only the way to Miriam's liberation, it was also to her own.

"I see the whole picture now, Miriam. I can appreciate your full greatness. I know that you entered my life to make a gift of your wisdom. I was blind for many years, I did you an injustice yet you accepted it. You remained true to yourself and that was your greatest gift. You knew your way and you never left it. I've now understood that. Not just my head but my heart also understands that. While my reason pondered solutions for the insoluble, you spoke to my soul. My soul has absorbed everything. It is all there. To start with I didn't even know that I have a soul. But now I do know and I will never again forget that. You dwell within me and all your treasures, the purity of your being will accompany me. I thank you for everything … have a safe journey to your new homeland, wherever it may be."

It did not take much strength to blow out the flame. A wisp of smoke rose from the wick. In it Valerie recognized the shape of a horse. The smoke cleared and an unexpected clarity filled the room.

"The air feels so pure," Valerie said.

She turned to the shaman, Evi, who was kneeling on the floor. "I would like to thank you for being so patient with me. I have often treated you unjustly, I was distrustful and I judged you."

"Sometimes it takes a while before our eyes can be opened but once we've seen the truth we forget the darkness that lies behind us." The expression on Evi's face was mild, the hint of a smile passed across her pale cheeks.

"Thank you for everything that you've done for me."

"I did it willingly. And I say that with all my heart."

Valerie embraced the fragile Evi, then she took a step back. "If you need my help with the move ..."

"Can't do any harm," Evi said.

"I shall go home now," Valerie said and took her leave.

25

Where was 'home', Valerie asked herself after she had left Evi's house. It did not take her long to find the answer. As if on auto-pilot her hands turned the steering wheel in the direction of the stable. The car park in front of the barn was empty. The dung heap, the tractor, the field were all enveloped in the same loneliness that Valerie still felt. Not a concealed loneliness but an open wound. In the stable she walked down the aisle between the stalls until she reached Korbas.

The large, dark animal raised his head. Through the bars their eyes met. This time she did not turn away because of his unbearable suffering. She now recognized her own suffering in him. Events had united them. Korbas was suffering just as she was. He, too, had lost the only human being in his life. She opened the door and went into his stall. He inclined his heavy, formless head to her as if he had long been waiting for her.

"I'm here with you now, Korbas. Together we will make it."

It seemed to her that she glimpsed in the horse's eye light from a tear. She had seen a halter hanging on the stall door. "I don't even know how you put such a thing on, but I suppose I can try." She examined the construction made of broad woven material with a metal buckle. Korbas stood there patiently as if he was prepared to put up with even her hundredth attempt. At last Valerie found the opening for the head. She drew the strap over his ears and buckled it closed under his chin. She thought she heard Miriam's voice say: well done.

Valerie pushed open the stable door. "Come on," she said and Korbas took several tentative steps, unsure whether she was serious or not.

"Let's walk together for a bit," Valerie said. "It's better to walk than to stand around. We have to move, that's the main thing."

Korbas walked beside her, down the aisle, neither pushing her on nor lingering behind her. It filled Valerie with an unexpected feeling of happiness to feel the horse walking next to her as if he had some finely tuned sense of where to put his body to keep the right distance from her and to find the right speed: not too fast nor too slow.

She had no objective whatsoever with the horse, she was simply astonished that, wearing the halter, he was calmly walking beside her down the aisle. She opened the barn door, the horse stepped out into the open and stopped behind her.

Valerie caught sight of his hooves, she had always been afraid of horses' hooves, but these aroused no fear in her. Everything she had ever thought about horses was overlain with the feeling that she and Korbas had suffering in common. Instead of a threat she felt security, as if he now provided the place where she could find that.

Ahead of them lay fields surrounded by wooded hills enclosing the farm on three sides. A path wound its way up the slope.

"It'll be good to go into the forest," Valerie said. "Do you want to go there with me? I think I would feel good there." The horse took a few steps and Valerie followed him. As if they had a common purpose they followed the path up the hill and eventually reached the edge of the forest. The lights dancing on the leaves and branches captivated them completely. It was as if they were setting off together into a new life in which the simplest things were miraculous: a stream bubbling along to the right of the path, a mushroom opening like a fan half way up a tree trunk, a falcon circling over a forest clearing.

I feel as if I were at the centre of the world, Valerie thought. Completely still and completely protected. As if I knew the secret law of all things. And Korbas felt the same.

Each time Valerie had reached the end of a path, she waited to see which direction Korbas would take, then she followed him. They penetrated deeper and deeper into the forest and she did not doubt for a single moment that Korbas was well disposed towards her. After a while it occurred to her that they were heading back towards the stable. Probably horses instinctively looked for the way back, at least that was what Miriam had often told her.

Up to this point they had not met anybody else but now Valerie felt that Korbas had sensed something. He lifted his head and his ears went up. They could already see the edge of the forest, then a figure appeared at the end of the path.

"Tom!"

The horse's pace quickened.

"How did you find me?" she asked with astonishment.

"I was on my way to Evi's. Then I saw your car parked at the farm. I saw that Korbas' box was empty and found fresh droppings on the path. It's called tracking."

"You've come to say good-bye, right? This is the day for good-byes."

"Come and visit me on the new farm," Tom said and smiled broadly. "We'll have very beautiful horses there. I've found a half-sister of Gitanes' and I have brought the frozen semen of a beautiful male mustang with me." His eyes glowed. Horses meant everything to him. He really loved them. And now that she understood this love for horses slightly better, the reserve she had felt towards him had vanished.

"I'd very much like to visit you," Valerie said. "In the future I will certainly need all the tips about horses that I can get. And anyway I have to see Gitanes again, and of course meet his relatives."

It flashed through Valerie's mind: I am no longer alone. There are not only Tom and Evi and Gitanes and Korbas, there were also her friends in Arizona, Salik, Lauren, Donna … The veil of loneliness was torn open. She felt profound love for these people who had come into her life because of Miriam's death.

"I always thought that I could explain the secret of life with my intellect, that intellect is the measure of all things," Valerie said, "and no one could tell me otherwise. Until a medicine horse named Gitanes entered my life. Until I got to know the wisdom of horses." She looked up at Korbas. "Horses have taught me that there is something else, something wonderful that I would like to get to know better." The look in Korbas' eyes penetrated to the very depths of her soul.

"My new life has only just begun."

They followed the path that led them out of the forest.

"I now believe that I have a future after all," Valerie said. "Even if for a long time it did not seem so."

ABOUT THIS BOOK

Invisible Networks
Books have a way of spinning an invisible web—and the other way round: an invisible web has its way of seeking out a poor author—in this case me—so that a particular book can find its way into the hands of particular readers.

It began with Gitanes
"Your next horse is called Gitanes and he is a paint horse," this was the sentence my Arab mare and soul mate Tinnia whispered to me one day. Gitanes is French for gypsy. At that time, however, there was no room in my life for an additional horse. But at least I was able to write about one.

Initiation
Three months later in Arizona, USA, I had an initiation experience which changed my view of things—and my whole life—forever. Horses played the decisive role in that; I began to see their remarkable abilities as healers, teachers and soul mates.

The death of a child
A short time later I dreamt the story for this book and the following morning wrote it down. When I read my e-mails, I found one from a fellow writer telling me about her son's death, exactly as I had dreamt it. Two months later I told my British riding friend, Rosie, about the story I had started to write in the meantime and she told me of her German friend, Sabine, who had experienced exactly the same events.

She had lost her daughter in a car crash and was now saddled with a horse called Giddy and a life in shreds, but which—as she put it—"with God's help and her Christian faith is now very happy again." Sabine was prepared to talk to me about her feelings, and I would like here to express my sincere gratitude to her, because through her I gained more profound access to the story.

Gypsy horses

I took another year for me to complete the first draught of the story and a further year to revise it. In the meantime I got to know Isabella Sonntag, the Wu Wei Verlag publisher (*wu-wei-verlag.com*) and her stallion Zingaro. Zingaro is Portuguese and also means 'gypsy', like Gitanes, the central horse in my novel. Zingaro had appeared to Isabella in a dream after she had read my book *On the Wings of Horses*, which is about intuitive communication with horses. The next day in a stable in Portugal Isabella found Zingaro standing before her in the flesh. And now he adorns her publishing house calendar. He is an award-winning stallion and is already well on the way to becoming a star.

The same year Esther Kochte, a prominent authoress und consciousness trainer (thetafloating.com), I had had the pleasure of meeting, bought a stallion called Gitano (Spanish for 'gypsy'), and I got to know the highly sensitive Gitana (the feminine variant of Gitano) on Almut von Döllen's farm in the Black Forest. (nestjockelhof.de).

Gypsy horses in many languages.

In the meantime I had myself become a gypsy. I travelled from farm to farm throughout Germany, Norway, France and Arizona in the USA, introducing people to the spirit of horses as healers and teachers.

I decided to develop the Medicine Horse idea into a series, in order to narrate stories from the very centre of my life and experience with horses, stories in which horses reveal unknown worlds to us, and in which threatening and inexplicable feelings and perceptions acquire a therapeutic meaning.

The Cover

The text was eventually finished and I set off in search of a cover illustration. When I discovered the portrait "One with the wind" on www.spiritofhorse.com, the website of the American horse painter Kim McElroy, I knew: that's it! I asked her if she would give me the legal right to use the picture for the cover. Kim McElroy informed me that the owner of the horse had asked her not to release the rights for commercial purposes. The picture had been painted for Alicia as a tribute to her beloved horse, Casanova, and the pain of losing him was still too great. Kim McElroy offered me various other wonderful covers but I was certain that it had to be this one. I wrote Kim an e-mail which she forwarded to Alicia, to explain that the book was about mourning and about how horses can help us overcome that. Alicia answered me in the following words: "I have to say that when I read about the content of your book my hair stood on end. I lost my fiancé, the love of my life, in a motorcycle accident and— to put it mildly—I was totally wiped out inwardly. I bought Casanova shortly after Jeff's death and the horse was all I had. He was the only reason I had for getting out of bed in the morning. I have always told Cas that he is the very best medicine in existence.

How fitting the title *Medicine Horse* is! The more I discover about the book the more suitable it seems to me that Cas should be on the cover."
I wish to thank Alicia und Kim with all my heart for granting me the rights to the picture. Not only books, but horses too have their way of spinning invisible webs.

The Readers
In my experience books also have a way of falling into the hands of certain readers, and continuing to weave webs in their lives. I, the author, my philanthropic horses, the visible and the invisible ones, have done their job.
Now it is your turn...

All the very best.
Ulrike Dietmann
Kirchheim, January 2012

About the Author

Ulrike Dietmann, born 1961, studied "scenic writing" at the Berlin University of the Arts and has published numerous dramatic works, radio plays, novels, translations and non-fiction. She runs a creative writing school; and after training with Linda Kohanov has for many years been working as an Eponaquest Instructor in personal development with horses. Her most prominent teaching model is the Hero`s Journey, that she teaches internationally. She lives with her family in the Stuttgart area.

Visit her websites:
www.spirithorse.info
www.pegasus-schreibschule.de
www.ulrikedietmann.de

Ulrike
Dietmann

ON THE
WINGS OF
HORSES

A Hero's Journey into the Heart
of the Creature

A Book for You

Foreword by Linda Kohanov

Cover Art © Kim McElroy

Available at Amazon.com as print-
book or Kindle edition

Zeitfracht Medien GmbH
Ferdinand-Jühlke-Straße 7
99095 Erfurt, Deutschland
produktsicherheit@kolibri360.de